Soldier Without A Gun

Karen Whiting

First published in 2023 by Blossom Spring Publishing
Soldier Without A Gun © 2023 Karen Whiting
ISBN 978-1-7392326-5-8
E: admin@blossomspringpublishing.com
W: www.blossomspringpublishing.com

For my Great Grandfather, Arthur Richards, and all those who did not carry a gun but fought every day to save the lives of those who did.

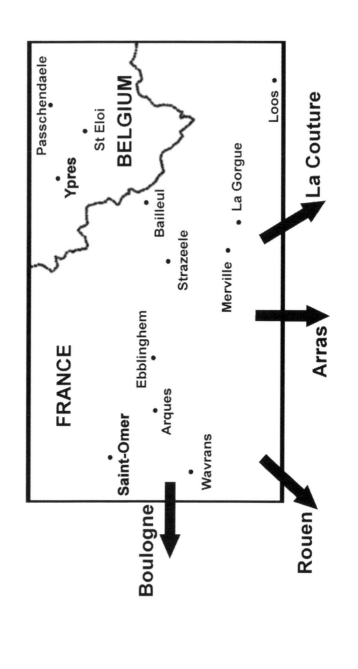

Chapter One

Harry woke to find himself sprawled on his bed, half-dressed, head pounding. The smell from the empty whisky bottle on the bedside table made him retch. It was still dark outside and the streetlamp in front of the house cast an amber glow through the open curtains, as if dawn were breaking. He hauled himself up and rested on the edge of the bed, fighting the waves of nausea. How had he even managed to get up to his bedroom last night?

It was several minutes before he felt able to negotiate the steep stairs. He lit the gas lamp and made his way into the kitchen, wincing as his feet hit the cold tiles. The tap squeaked and released a stream of icy water into the dirty sink. He leant forward and splashed his face, gasping and cursing with the shock. The squat range hadn't been lit for days and stood cold and desolate in the corner. He opened the larder door and recoiled at the foul stench, the culprit a half-empty bottle of milk. Holding his breath, he poured the contents away, the rancid lumps splashing into the sink. He checked the larder again and retrieved the remains of a stale loaf and a pot of jam. Tearing off a piece of bread, he dipped it in the jar and scooped up some of the preserve. He half expected his stomach to reject the sickly sweetness but in fact the nausea subsided. He plodded through to the front room and dropped into the nearest armchair where he continued to dunk the dried-out bread, staring at the floor. He had to pull himself together. Start with a bit of cleaning, maybe. But then again, what was the point?

The room was a jumble of discarded clothing and half-eaten meals. Even through the reek of stale cigarette smoke, he could detect a tang coming off the unwashed garments. Crumbs and embers spilling over from the remains of an old fire littered the faded rug and an ashtray brimming with cigarette stubs lay surrounded by abandoned cups and glasses. A photograph of his mother and father, dressed in their finery, nestled amongst the clutter. Harry noticed the date of a ring-stained newspaper. Two months old. Huh. Was it that long ago? The last time the outside world had been of any interest to him?

As daylight seeped through the curtains, Harry heaved himself out of the chair and ventured a glance in the mirror above the mantlepiece. He didn't recognise the image staring back at him. His hair was greasy and unkempt. Dark circles under his eyes drained his face of colour and stubble was appearing on his jawline and chin. What a mess. He could smell his own body but couldn't summon up the energy to light the range and heat enough water to fill the tin bath which was propped against the wall outside the back door, untouched for two weeks. He opted instead to sluice himself down at the kitchen sink and drag a comb through his matted hair. The stubble would have to stay.

Upstairs, the wardrobe thankfully revealed a solitary clean shirt which he snatched off the hanger then slammed the doors shut. The sight of his wedding suit hanging forlornly alongside Mary's dresses was too much to bear. Hearing voices in the street, he peered out of the window. It was the Garbutts over the road saying goodbye to their eldest. Harry watched the son hug his mother and shake hands with his father, then pick up his case and stride down the street with the confidence of someone heading off on an adventure. Mr Garbutt put his arm around his wife's shoulders as she wept into a handkerchief, his face a mixture of pride and dread as he watched his boy disappear round the corner.

So many had enlisted now. He would hear the newspaper sellers heralding the latest news from the

Front and he'd driven past the snaking queues of eager men waiting outside the recruiting office. Friends and acquaintances had joined the rush, seduced by the patriotic fervour and keen to serve their country. It had been widely believed the war would be over within a matter of months and he'd made no apologies for ignoring the call to arms. There were plenty of unmarried men to fight for the cause. As it turned out, the prediction of an early victory had been wildly optimistic and the battle across the Channel was still raging.

Several minutes later, he stepped out of the front door. He realised his neighbours were leaving too. Why hadn't he checked the coast was clear?

"Oh, Mr Stone. Good morning. How nice to see you."

"Morning Mrs Miller. Mr Miller." Harry doffed his cap and saw a flash of shock cross his neighbours' face. He obviously hadn't cleaned up as well as he thought. The woman was slight with a thin face, but bright-eyed and she quickly resumed her friendly smile. Mr Miller was a stout man with dark hair and a neat moustache.

"Will we see you in church on Sunday, Mr Stone?" he asked. Not a chance.

"Not sure, Mr Miller."

"It might help, you know?"

Harry forced a weak smile, willing the couple to leave. It was weeks since he had last attended service and he had found little comfort in the dreary sermons. Mary had been the regular churchgoer and he the hanger-on. He had accompanied her because he knew it made her happy. These days he couldn't face the looks of pity he received from half the members of the congregation and disapproval for his absence from the other half.

"I'll tell the Reverend to expect you next Sunday then." The neighbour turned up his collar and ushered his wife along the path. She turned and called back.

3

"I'm making stew, Mr Stone. I'll drop some round for you."

Harry felt a rush of gratitude at the thought of home-cooked food. He checked his pocket watch and realised he was going to be late for work.

**

The hour was too early for shoppers, but the roads were busy. An omnibus packed with men in uniform rumbled past. They were talking and laughing, and Harry caught the sound of singing mixed with the hubbub. He couldn't really see what they had to be happy about. The January air was bitter, and an icy wind cut into him. He hastened through the streets, passing several newspaper stands plastered with reports of the sinking of HMS Formidable by a German submarine.

A short while later, he turned into the cobbled yard of A.E. Williams Provisions Merchants. Harry had secured a position as delivery driver a year earlier when the storekeeper had invested in the latest motorised van, dispensing with the traditional horse and cart. The van was parked on the cobbles, rear doors open wide, and Mr Williams himself was lugging crates and boxes into the back. Harry approached and muttered an apology.

Williams continued loading. "Late again, Harry. Third time this week."

"Yes, Sir. Sorry."

Williams slammed the doors shut and turned to face him. His eyes opened wide with shock, and he ran his hand through his hair in frustration. "Heavens, lad, did you look in a mirror this morning?"

Harry's colour came up and he looked down at his feet, embarrassment choking any words of reply. The storekeeper sighed and softened his tone. "Right, get

4

yourself tidied up a bit before you start the round, then crack on."

"Yes, Sir."

***

Ten minutes later Harry was behind the wheel and crawling in the slow-moving traffic. He was sandwiched between two horse-drawn carts, one loaded with milk churns and the other barrels of beer. The pavements were now dotted with the first pedestrians brave enough to face the cold wind gusting through the streets, whipping the women's long skirts round their ankles and whisking the men's hats away.

He followed the queue west along Broad Street, like a procession without any spectators, inching past the terracotta façade of Reading's department store. He glanced up at the ornate frontage, its balustrade and clockface dominated by the giant letters, Heelas, which balanced as if by magic on the rooftop. The last thing Harry had purchased there was his wedding suit. It had taken months of saving. He wanted the money to go on Mary's dress, his suit didn't really matter, but she had insisted. He was never comfortable in formal clothing and even though his lean frame should have lent itself to a tailored look, the suit had hung awkwardly on him. Mary had tried to hide a smile as he stood in front of her.

"You look very handsome," she had said, with a twinkle in her eye, as she reached up to plant a kiss on his cheek.

The two lanes of traffic separated to negotiate a bronze statue standing tall on its granite plinth in the centre of the road. George Palmer, casually holding his hat and umbrella in his right hand, his lapel in his left and smiling down on the townsfolk. Huntley and Palmer had been his

5

father's employers for his entire working life and had provided Harry with a job after leaving school at thirteen. The factory and its yards had been Harry's world where he carried out any task asked of him with gusto and earned the affection of workers and management alike. It was also where he had learned to drive.

Several drop-offs later, Harry pulled up outside an elegant town house set back from the road. A long, straight path divided the front garden and led the way to a glossy door with polished brass numbers. He jumped down, rubbing his hands against the cold, and scooted to the rear of the van where the doors were emblazoned with the shop name. Gold lettering on black paintwork. Williams had inherited the business from his father, Albert, and had transformed it from a small grocery store to a thriving merchant with a reputation in the town for quality goods and professional service. He unloaded a crate stacked with groceries and followed the path through the manicured lawn and shrubs. As he bent to set the crate down, the door swung open and a smartly dressed woman with greying hair and thin lips stepped forward.

"Mr Stone! Where have you been?"

"My apologies, Mrs South. The traffic was heavy down Broad Street."

"This is the third week in a row."

"I know, Mrs South. Shall I carry it in?" Harry moved to pick up the crate, but the woman let out an exasperated cry.

"No, no, no. These aren't the groceries I ordered."

Harry looked down at the selection of goods and produce and sighed. "Are you sure, Mrs South?"

"Yes, Mr Stone. Very sure. I don't eat tinned tomatoes and I don't need sardines."

Harry stared at the crate as if its contents might

spontaneously transform themselves. "I must have picked up the wrong one, Mrs South. Back in a moment."

He lifted the box and hastened to the van, willing the correct order to be lurking somewhere amongst the crates and cases. But he already knew it wasn't going to be there. He'd deposited the previous delivery in a small shed in the back yard, according to the customer's instructions, but realised now he'd failed to double-check the name. He was in trouble now. It was going to be an hour's round trip to swap the crates and return. Harry cursed himself and made his way back up the path to the waiting Mrs South, now standing with her arms folded.

"Sorry, Mrs South. There's been a mix-up. I'll be back as quickly as I can."

"This can't carry on. I'm going to have to speak to Mr Williams."

The woman slammed the door, leaving him standing alone, a flurry of snowflakes dancing round him in the wind.

***

It was a long day of late deliveries and profuse apologies. The only relief was managing to avoid a confrontation with his employer, who had been busy with a customer when he finally pulled into the goods yard behind the shop. Mr Williams had signalled for him to wait, but Harry indicated he was in a hurry and dashed away before the shopkeeper could protest. He would face the stern words tomorrow.

He unlocked his front door and threw himself into the nearest armchair. For ten minutes he stared at the fireplace, averting his eyes from the black and white photograph perched on the narrow mantelpiece, but eventually the pull was too great, and he lifted his head.

He fixed his gaze on the happy image and began to sob.

Chapter Two

A fist hammered on the van door and Harry jumped in his seat. He tried to focus as a face appeared at the window, puce with anger.

"You're blocking the road, you half-wit!"

Holding a hand up by way of an apology, he shifted the van into gear and pulled over to the side of the road. He waved again as the furious driver edged round, throwing him one last bilious look. Harry screwed his eyes shut and let his head fall forward again, his hands clenched around the steering wheel, stretching the skin taut across his knuckles. The noises of the street blended into a single drone which forged its way into his brain like a drill, invasive and unrelenting. He had to find a way through this. Sort himself out. But he couldn't see a day when the shame and self-loathing would end.

Several minutes passed before he lifted his eyes. He had managed to avoid Williams again that morning, but with deliveries completed, it was time to face him. As he looked round to check for vehicles, his eyes were drawn to a large man, several yards away, yelling at a cowering sheepdog. The dog was skin and bone and shivering, with his tail between his legs. The man raised his walking stick and whipped it across the dog's rump, causing the dog to howl in pain. He yanked on the lead and the dog yelped. For Christ's sake. Harry leapt down from the cab and marched towards them.

"Hey, what the hell are you doing?"

The man looked round in surprise, then snarled, "Get lost." He lifted the stick again, but Harry grabbed his hand and tugged the stick from the man's grip.

"Don't do that."

The man squared up to him, now red with rage. "Mind your own business and piss off."

"And let you beat the shit out of your dog? Don't think so."

The man was about to throw a punch when his face broke into a smile. Harry was confused for a moment but sensed movement behind him and turned to see a figure even larger than the dog owner, a wall of bone and muscle with a bald head and several missing teeth.

"You haven't met my brother," said the first man, with a sneer.

"What's going on here, then?" asked the brother, starting to roll up his sleeves.

"I was just stopping this idiot from beating a helpless animal," replied Harry, giving the brute a grin. The man straightened to his full height, his eyes gleaming with the anticipation of a fight.

"Who are you calling an idiot?" He began to punch his fist into the palm of his other hand. "You must have a death wish or something."

Harry looked at the terrified dog then at the brother.

"Perhaps you're right," he said and landed the first punch.

***

Sitting on the dirty floor, Harry stared at the wall, trying to decipher the scratched messages left by aggrieved prisoners. It had been a cold and uncomfortable night, listening to the ranting and swearing of drunk and angry inmates in the neighbouring cells whilst nursing a split lip and black eye. The only problem now was his boss. Had he been out looking for him? He must be wondering where he and the delivery van were. His job had been hanging by a thread, but this would be the end. He heard the bolt shifting on his cell door and stood up. The stern-faced policeman who'd locked him up, appeared.

"You're free to go," he said.

Harry picked up his cap and silently followed the officer through to the custody area where he was handed two sets of keys, his wallet, and his pocket watch.

"If I catch you brawling in the street again, you'll be spending more than a night in the nick, do you hear?"

Harry pocketed his belongings and emerged from the sombre lighting of the police station, squinting in the sunlight of another frosty day. He would have hurried back to the van if he thought it would make any difference, but his fate was sealed, so he walked through the streets to the scene of the brawl. The van was where he'd left it, unscathed. He climbed up into the cab and drove steadily back to the shop.

***

Williams had heard the engine and was storming across the yard before Harry had even turned the engine off.

"Where the bloody hell have you been?" he said. Harry lowered himself down.

"In the nick."

"The nick? What the hell for?"

"Fighting."

Williams clutched his head with his hands. "And where was the van?"

"On the Oxford Road."

"All night?"

Harry nodded. "There's no damage. I checked."

"Jesus, Harry. This can't carry on." Williams paced up and down, rubbing his brow while Harry watched. He knew what was coming. After a minute, the storekeeper stopped and turned to him. "Listen, I know you've hit hard times, lad, and I feel for you, I really do, but I'm going to have to let you go. I can't make allowances for you anymore."

Harry dropped his head. He couldn't blame the man.

"I'll get you your wages," said Williams.

He waited while the storekeeper disappeared into the stockroom at the back of the shop. If it were possible, his joyless existence had just plummeted into an even darker place. For a moment, he considered pleading with his employer, but he'd be making promises he knew he wouldn't keep. Who would employ him now? Williams returned moments later with a small, brown envelope.

"I've paid you what I owe you and added a little extra to tide you over."

"Thank you," said Harry, taking the envelope.

"Piece of advice, lad. Stop drinking and stop getting into fights." With that, Williams stepped back into the building and closed the door behind him.

***

The flurry of snow the previous day had come to nothing, so the paths were clear, but the air was even more bitter. Harry's head was in a blur. What was he going to do? Mary would have been disappointed in him. Who would take him on now? Would he have to sell the house? The thought sent a surge of dread through him.

He arrived at his front door and slotted the key in the lock but didn't turn it. What was waiting for him inside? Dirty pots, unwashed clothes and flashbacks to the day that destroyed his life. And he needed a drink. He withdrew the key and retraced his steps back into town.

As he drifted along the familiar streets, he followed the road curving round Forbury Gardens. Deciding to cut through the park, he weaved his way around the lacework of paths, passing the memorial, and emerged onto Valpy Street. He continued up the road until he saw the

Boar Inn.

Stepping into the warm, smoky atmosphere, Harry crossed the flagstone floor to the bar. A few lunchtime drinkers were dotted around including three youths with filthy faces and clothing, grouped in a corner. One of them had pockmarked skin and blackened teeth. All eyes were on Harry.

"Whisky, please."

The landlord was short with a generous paunch protruding over the top of his once-white apron. He placed a glass on the counter and poured a tot. Harry threw back the whisky and ordered another. He pulled out the envelope from his pocket and emptied some of the change onto the bar.

"Tell me when I've used this up."

The landlord poured another measure and watched Harry down it immediately.

"Easy, lad," he said.

In the corner the three men were nudging each other. They sat quietly sipping their beer and watching Harry knocking back glass after glass.

Half an hour later, Harry produced a crumpled cigarette and patted himself in search of a light. He tried to focus. "Got a match?" His words were starting to slur, and the room was spinning. He staggered to one side and grabbed the bar to steady himself.

"Think you've had enough, lad," said the landlord. Harry was about to protest but his stomach sent a wave of nausea to his throat. He got the door in his sights and took a shaky step towards it. Aware of movement across the room, a moment later he felt an arm around his shoulder. "C'mon, mate. We'll give you a hand."

He tried to shrug off the man, but two more figures appeared by his side and guided him through the door and out onto the street. He gave them a couple of drunken shoves but realised one of them was digging into his trouser pocket. They were going for his wages.

"Get your hands off me, you bastards," he snarled. The one with the bad skin and teeth gave a victory wave with the brown envelope. Harry snatched at it, but he was too slow.

"Don't think so, mate," said the ringleader.

Harry felt a surge of anger and jabbed the grinning youth on the nose, jerking his head back with a crack. Blood trickled from his nostril and the look of shock on his face turned to fury. He stepped forward and punched Harry hard in the stomach. Harry grunted in pain and retched, tasting whisky and bile. He straightened up and found himself with his arms pinned behind his back. A fist slammed into his face, and he dropped to his knees, ears ringing. Another blow to his head sent him sprawling across the pavement and the last thing he remembered was the sound of running feet echoing down the street.

***

He came round on the floor of the pub, propped awkwardly against the bar. A blanket had been laid over him. He recognised the landlord's voice and someone else was there. Someone in a dark uniform.

"He's coming round."

"Get a damp cloth for that lip."

Harry's vision gradually cleared and for the second time that day he was looking into the face of a policeman.

"You alright, lad?"

He tried to shift position, but his head was throbbing, and a dull ache stretched across his middle. Couldn't be better.

"What's your name, son?"

"They took my money, the bastards," said Harry. A

cool cloth was placed against his cheek, and he tasted blood.

"I've taken a description from Percy here," said the policeman, nodding at the landlord. "What's your name?"

"Harry. Harry Stone."

"Right, Harry. First things first, let's get you home. Is there someone there who can keep an eye on you?"

Harry shook his head, wincing. "I'm fine."

"Not sure you are," replied the officer.

Harry hauled himself up, gasping with pain. "Really, I'm fine. I can walk."

"I need to take your details, son."

"Won't make any difference. They're long gone."

The policeman tried to help him, but Harry shrugged him off. "Just leave me be."

"I really think you need a bit of help," said the officer, but Harry just waved him away. He shuffled out of the pub and made his way painfully towards home.

Chapter Three

For two days, Harry existed in a fog of whisky and self-pity. He closed the curtains and ignored any knocking at the front door. All he wanted to do was forget. Forget he no longer had a wife. Forget he no longer had a job. When he wasn't staring at his wedding photograph, he would study the picture of his parents, wondering what they would think of him now.

Harry had been born on a wintry night in mid-December. It was a straightforward birth, and his father didn't have long to wait before he heard the cry of his second son coming from the bedroom above. Cradling the new-born with his wife, Rachel, smiling at him from the bed and his eldest still fast asleep, John Stone felt his life was complete.

Harry's parents had met in the summer of 1887, a chance encounter outside the gates of Huntley and Palmer. In his rush to get home John had attempted a running jump onto his bicycle and ended up sprawled at the feet of a passer-by. As he looked up, he found himself gazing into the face of a young woman.

"Are you alright?" she said, stifling a laugh.

John scrabbled to his feet and retrieved his cap, noticing his workmates were cycling into the distance, guffawing at his mishap. Pink with embarrassment, he brushed himself down.

"Yes, thank you," he said and bent to pick up his bicycle, now a mangled wreck with a buckled wheel and twisted handlebar.

"Oh, dear," said the woman, still trying to keep a straight face.

He eyed the bent metal and began to laugh. Now on foot and by way of apology, he offered to carry the woman's basket and accompany her home.

John had proposed in a matter of weeks, despite having nowhere to live. Beguiled by the romance of the swift proposal, a maiden aunt had generously gifted them the funds to purchase a property where they could set up home. Ronald was born less than a year later, Harry eleven months after that and, supported by John's income from his employment at the factory, the family lived a contented life.

But Harry's memories of his early years were now hazy and distant, obscured by the events of a day in the spring of 1896. The boys had been warned repeatedly to stay away from the canal at the end of their road, but Ron had created a new game which needed the waterway as a backdrop and Harry had made no objection, happy to follow his brother's lead. All it had taken was a stumble and Ronald had tumbled into the murky water and disappeared. Harry had called his name over and over, panic and terror engulfing him. He was about to launch himself in when a hand grabbed him and pulled him away from the edge.

"Stay back, lad," said a voice.

Harry watched as a man lowered himself into the water and dived into the blackness. It seemed an eternity before he emerged holding a limp and colourless Ronald.

Harry hid the tragedy of that day in a dark recess of his mind, but he remembered the change in his parents and that life was never the same again. A sadness had descended on the house, like a dense fog. Unable to comfort each other, his father had become distant and withdrawn, his mother permanently preoccupied and distracted. Harry would find her staring into space, clutching something of Ronald's, but when he tugged on her skirt, she would smile and give him the tightest hug. She still loved him. He wasn't so sure about his father. Harry wondered if he blamed him in some way and yearned to ask him. He never did, too afraid of the answer.

John and Rachel died of tuberculosis when Harry was seventeen. He continued to live in the family home, comfortable amongst his parents' belongings. It was where he had brought Mary after they were married and where they had planned their future together.

***

He took another swig of whisky and decided he could no longer ignore the searing hunger emanating from his empty stomach. Searching the house for coins, he turned out pockets and checked under cushions. Eventually he found some pennies in the drawer of a dresser. A glance in the mirror revealed the skin around his eye was now a vivid mauve with yellow edges. His lip was less swollen, and the cut was healing. Purple bruising had appeared across his stomach, but he was able to move without flinching. He peeked through the curtains to make sure none of his neighbours were in sight, then slipped out of the door, locked it quickly, and, pulling his cap low over his eyes, hastened up the street. His destination was a bakery. His plan, to buy as much bread as the change would fund and be back home in ten minutes. He wished he had enough to buy a bottle of whisky.

To his relief, the shop was empty of customers. He could see the shopkeeper eyeing his beaten face, but once Harry placed the money on the counter, the man relaxed and took the order. Harry grabbed the package and mumbled his thanks. He was barely out of the shop before he'd ripped a piece of bread from the loaf and stuffed it in his mouth. Wincing as the cut on his lip protested, he turned for home, then instantly froze. Walking towards him was Mary's mother and sister. As he hesitated, he saw his mother-in-law's expression shift from recognition, to shock, then contempt. He had to get away. He spun round and collided with an elderly couple, sending the woman teetering sideways and his bread to the ground.

"I'm so sorry," he said.

The man steadied his wife and guided her round Harry. "Pay more attention to where you're going, young man."

"Yes, Sir." Harry bent down to retrieve his supplies. As he rose, Mary's mother was standing before him, her eyes dark and forbidding. He shoved the bag of bread in his pocket and removed his cap. This was going to be bad.

"Good morning, Mrs Fisher. Good morning, Miss Fisher," he said.

"How dare you," said the older woman, her eyes blazing. "Greeting me as if all is well in the world."

For a moment Harry thought she was going to strike him. He swallowed and scrunched his cap in his hand.

"Where have you been? Hiding away like the coward you are?"

"Mother, please," said her daughter, a look of embarrassment flashing across her face.

"No, Eleanor. He must be told. Was the guilt too much for you? Skulking away from your wife's funeral…my daughter's funeral."

Harry felt his eyes prick with tears and lowered his head. There was nothing he could say. No excuse. The woman continued. "You failed her. You failed her as a husband, and you failed her as her protector. And have no doubt, God will judge you." With that, she brushed past him and continued along the path, leaving the smell of her sickly perfume hanging in the air. Eleanor stepped forward and rested her gloved hand on his sleeve.

"Don't listen to her. She's grieving and she's angry."

"She's right though isn't she?" said Harry.

She patted his arm and hurried after her mother.

Harry felt his knees begin to buckle and stumbled to the edge of the pavement, where he collapsed onto the curb and dropped his head into his hands.

Everything the woman had said was true. He had failed Mary and she had paid the price. By the day of the funeral, any strength he may have had remaining evaporated the minute he saw Mary's coffin. It was all he could do to get through the service. Accepting condolences and engaging in polite conversation was beyond him. And so, he had escaped.

A horse and cart trotted past, the driver yelling a warning as the wheel nearly clipped Harry's foot. He hauled himself up and gazed around, pedestrians dodging round him with a tut or a huff. He was lost. Adrift in a sea of guilt and despair without purpose or direction. What was to become of him?

An omnibus trundled by with the stern face of Lord Kitchener adorning the side and as Harry's eyes followed it, Kitchener's finger appeared to be pointing directly at him.

Chapter Four

The motor bus passed through the gateway into the sprawling barracks and came to a juddering halt on the edge of a large parade ground. The recruits spilled out into the open space, taking in the frenetic activity around them. Military vehicles coming and going, soldiers marching and army personnel dashing between buildings. They were instructed to line up by a short, wiry sergeant with a thin moustache and receding hair. Harry sensed the mixture of excitement and nerves within the group. Despite the chill, he was sweating under his overcoat. He tugged at his shirt collar and adjusted his hat. Every volunteer was dressed in his best suit with a small case at his feet. He felt a nudge from the man next to him, who nodded towards an officer striding across the parade ground, baton in hand. Coming to a halt in front of the group, the officer tucked his baton under his arm and stepped forward.

"Welcome to Aldershot, gentlemen. My name is Captain Roberts, and this is Sergeant Moore. Sergeant Moore will be guiding you through your training, making sure you are fighting fit and ready for action. I'll tell you now, you'll have some tough days ahead of you, but I can assure you, the army will equip you with all the skills you need to fight and defeat the enemy. Good luck, gentlemen." The captain gave a cursory nod to the Sergeant and marched away. Moore cleared his throat.

"Right, you lot, follow me. I'll show you to your quarters. You'll have fifteen minutes to unpack and then, gentlemen, time for a short, back and sides."

The men followed Moore through the warren of low buildings. They were shown into a sparse dormitory with a row of bunks either side, each with a slim wardrobe and a locker. Harry made a beeline for a bed at the far end of the room, hoping to keep any conversation to a minimum. Aware of a suitcase dropping on to the neighbouring bunk he turned to see a smart, dark-haired man in his late thirties holding out his hand. He had soft, brown eyes and a friendly smile.

"Arthur Richards. Pleased to meet you."

They shook hands.

"Harry. Harry Stone."

"Where're you from Harry?"

"Reading."

"Ah, home of the famous biscuit."

Harry had already returned to the job of unpacking and didn't respond. Arthur was momentarily taken aback but gave a little shrug and turned his attention to the other recruits, shaking hands and exchanging names.

Moore was true to his word and a quarter of an hour later the recruits were instructed to follow him out and round a corner to join a queue of men waiting for a haircut. Suddenly conscious of his overgrown locks, uncut for months, Harry attempted to flatten the messy thatch. When his turn came, he sat down and the barber wrapped a sheet around him, tucking it into his collar. The clippers made short work of the cut and within minutes Harry was running his hands over his scalp, thinking they all looked more like soldiers already.

***

Supper was a greasy stew topped with tasteless dumplings. Harry positioned himself in a far corner of the mess and though he caught Arthur glancing across at him, managed to avoid eye contact. He just wanted to be left alone.

When he returned to the dormitory, despite the men having been advised to turn in early, someone had initiated a game of cards. Arthur raised his arm to get Harry's attention.

"Fancy trying your luck?"

"No, thanks," replied Harry, making for his bunk. He lit a cigarette and lay listening to the chatter. A group of strangers brought together in an unfamiliar place by a common cause.

***

The first day of training began early with reveille at five thirty. The men hurriedly dressed, most of them groggy after a fitful night on the hard bunks. They tidied their beds and gulped down a mug of tea. Harry cursed when he realised, he was last to join the group on the parade ground, earning a disapproving look from Moore. The sky was overcast and threatened rain, possibly even sleet. They rubbed their arms and blew into their hands, hopping from foot to foot. There followed an hour of star jumps, sprinting, press-ups, and jogging.

The relief was palpable when Moore called for a halt and directed them to breakfast. Harry devoured the bread and jam and washed it down with the ubiquitous mug of tea. His legs were already aching, and he could smell his own sweat.

Back on the parade ground they had the first taste of army drilling. They marched and turned about and marched some more, the sergeant roaring endless instructions. Anyone who fell behind or out of step was targeted immediately and suffered several minutes of Moore bellowing at close quarters. Lunch break couldn't come quickly enough. Harry removed himself from the crowd once again and chose a seat in the farthest corner.

***

It was a weary troop that filed into the dormitory that evening. Harry undressed and crawled under the sheets. He closed his eyes and thought about Mary. Would she be proud of him? He pictured her delicate face and smiling eyes. For the first time in months, he fell asleep before the happy image transformed into a nightmare.

**

One week into training, in the middle of supper, he spied Arthur approaching him and sighed with irritation.

"May I?" asked Arthur.

Harry shrugged. Probably couldn't avoid him for ever. Arthur took a seat and tucked into his food, grimacing as he tasted the pie.

"Tough day, eh?"

Harry nodded, chewing the stringy meat.

"Feet are killing me," said Arthur. "God bless the man who came up with the idea of route marches. Dreading taking my boots off."

Harry had been thinking the same thing.

"What line of work are you in?" asked Arthur.

"Delivery driver."

Arthur raised his eyebrows. "I'm a driver too — chauffeur."

Harry stopped eating and looked up at him. "What do you drive?"

"Rover Clegg 12."

"Very nice."

"Third gear's a bugger to find, though."

Harry gave a little laugh. "I drive vans. Every gear's hard to find."

The two of them finished their meal then walked back to their quarters together. As they stepped into the dormitory, they were met with a chorus of groans and swearing.

"Jesus, look at the size of this blister," said a young redhead called Charlie, lifting his foot in the air for all to see. The men were easing off their heavy boots and peeling away blood-soaked socks. Harry noticed a couple of them had somehow tracked down large bowls and were steeping their battered feet, the water turning a pale pink colour.

"Really, lads. Don't know what all the fuss is about," said Arthur, flopping down on his bed. He unlaced his boots and whipped off the left one, letting out a howl of pain. His face turned scarlet and as he flung his boot to the ground, the room erupted into laughter.

***

On an evening in late March, the men were sitting outdoors cleaning kit and smoking. Winter appeared to be over, and spring had brought milder air. Harry was polishing his boots and Arthur was writing home. As usual, talk was of the war. Some of the men had fathers and brothers already fighting. Charlie had been quietly listening but then spoke up.

"We got word in January about me Pa." The conversation died down. "Hit by a shell in his trench. Died instantly, they said."

Harry stopped polishing and studied the young recruit, who was staring at the ground. "It was time for me to step up. Me Ma didn't want me to, of course. Begged me not to come. Said the family had sacrificed enough." Charlie paused. "I 'ad to though. You lot understand." He said it as a statement rather than a question.

Arthur gave the young man a pat on the shoulder. "You're a brave lad. Your Pa would be proud of you." The men murmured agreement. Arthur scanned the sombre faces and pulled out a pack of cards from his pocket. "Anyone fancy a game of poker?"

Chapter Five

The following morning, with spring sunshine warming the back of his head, Harry was lying on his front peering through the sight of a Lee Enfield rifle. He focussed on a wooden figure a hundred yards away, held his breath and gently pulled the trigger. The bullet found its target and Harry allowed himself a little smile.

"Nice shot, Stone," said a voice behind him.

"Thank you, Sarge." He ran his hand along the smooth, polished wood, picturing himself heading over the top, charging the enemy, bayonet fixed. He longed for that day. He would be first up that ladder and first to cross No-man's Land. He had nothing to lose. Fate would decide if he lived or died.

Arthur was next in the row of shooters. He was fumbling with the bolt and swearing under his breath. Harry had noticed that none of Arthur's shots had been on target, and he watched as Arthur tried again and missed. The recruit on the far side of him snorted.

"Blimey, Richards, think we'd be better off if you were fighting for the other side."

A chuckle went down the line and Arthur muttered an expletive.

Harry leant towards him. "Don't worry. You'll get it. Take your time and hold your breath when you pull the trigger."

***

That evening, Harry found Arthur alone in the dormitory, lying on his bunk studying some small photographs. He dropped on to his bunk and thought for a moment, then said,

"May I see?"

Arthur sat up in surprise, then eagerly handed him a black and white picture of a petite woman with dark, curly hair. She was sitting in a garden with a shawl wrapped round her.

"My Flo."

Harry studied it then took the next one Arthur offered. Six little faces stared up at him and the family likeness struck him instantly.

"Right. Who's who?"

Arthur moved across and perched next to him. "That's Lily at the back, the eldest. Eleven. Mable next to her. Seven. Then Bill, he's eight. In front that's Nellie, five, Elsie, four and Harry, two."

Harry could detect the pride in Arthur's voice. "They look a handful," he said.

"Harry's certainly a little monkey. Bit worried about Bill. Think he misses me more than the others." Arthur was quiet for a moment. "Flo keeps them in order though. She's a tough little bird."

Harry pictured the family waiting for this kind-hearted father and husband to come home.

***

As spring made way for summer the men became increasingly impatient to be deployed. No longer raw recruits with pasty faces, they were bronzed and trim. They looked and felt like soldiers. Their leather boots had finally softened, and the blisters had healed. They could march for miles and drill all morning without a word of rebuke from Sergeant Moore.

On a scorching hot day with a cloudless sky above them and the sun bouncing off the parade ground, the men were doing morning drill — dripping with sweat and willing it to be over, Harry noticed even Sergeant Moore was pink in the face with beads of perspiration dotting his forehead. Out of the corner of his eye he spotted a figure approaching across the open space and a moment later an officer he didn't recognise stood facing them. The sergeant brought the men to attention.

"At ease, men," began the officer. "You are nearing completion of your basic training and I know you must be chomping at the bit to get into the action. Most of you will be continuing as infantry soldiers, however some of you, we know, have skills the Army can utilise, and we will be deploying those men to wherever you are needed the most."

The officer continued, "Step forward if you have training or experience in any of the following: mechanical, electrical or civil engineering."

Half a dozen men split from the ranks and gathered alongside the officer.

"Step forward if you have any medical training." Two more men made their way to the front. Harry's heart sank.

"And step forward if you can drive a motor vehicle." A few more broke away, Arthur amongst them. He stole a glance down the line expecting Harry to be following but Harry avoided his gaze and stared ahead. No way. Driving would mean no gun, no front line, and no fighting.

The officer exchanged a few words with Moore then addressed the newly formed group. "Into line and follow me."

Harry's eyes followed the men as they disappeared into the maze of buildings and wondered how he would explain himself to Arthur. He had no intention of spending the war transporting supplies from here to there. Or worse, driving troops towards the Front and watching them head into battle without him. He was going to fight.

He was going to carry a gun.

Arthur joined him at supper, the unspoken question hanging between them. They ate in silence until eventually he spoke.

"You do know, there's no shame in helping the war effort in a different way? You're still a soldier."

"Not really. Not without a gun," said Harry.

"Don't be daft. Everyone's playing their part. We can't all be on the front line."

"But that's where I want to be. Where I'm meant to be."

"Listen, you have a skill the army needs. You should be proud to use it." Arthur stood and picked up his tray. "You know I'm right."

Harry dropped his knife and fork and watched him walk away.

Chapter Six

Within twenty-four hours, Harry and Arthur left infantry training behind and found themselves assigned to 419 Company of the Army Service Corps. After a restless night, Harry had presented himself to the office the following morning and declared his occupation. The officer had studied him for a moment then taken down his details. "Better late than never, Private."

The Mechanical Transport Division had a shortage of drivers and within a couple of days the men learned they were to be attached to the Royal Army Medical Corps driving ambulance cars.

"Motor ambulances! Well, this should be fun," said Arthur, rubbing his hands together.

Harry smiled at his enthusiasm. "Better than driving crates of bully beef around."

"You're not kidding. We're going to be in the thick of it, my friend."

"Wonder how much training we'll get?"

"Sounds like they're keen for us to get to France sooner rather than later. Speak any French?"

Harry shook his head. "*Bonjour* and *au revoir* is about it."

"Me too. As long as we can learn how to order a beer, eh?"

***

To their surprise, the focus of training was not on handling the heavy ambulance cars, but rather, as medics. They were issued with a thick textbook detailing the basics of first aid and sanitation and they familiarised themselves with the Chain of Evacuation for Casualties, the latest way of processing and treating the wounded at the Front. They spent the days applying bandages, strapping splints to broken bones and stemming mock wounds.

In the first week of August, the men finally got the news they were to be deployed and soon found themselves in the back of a noisy, boneshaker of a truck on its way to the Berkshire town of Hungerford. The sleepy community was now a staging post on the main route from London to the ports at Bristol, the embarkation point for mechanical transport divisions, and had been transformed into a mobilisation camp, a bustling hub of military vehicles and army personnel preparing to go to war.

Harry was immediately charmed by the quaint town. A mix of pretty cottages and whitewashed houses lined the high street with the redbrick clock tower of the town hall breaking up the skyline. At odds with the picturesque scene was the endless line of army trucks, parked in parallel at forty-five degrees to the road as far as the eye could see.

The transport pulled up outside the town hall and the men alighted, stretching stiff backs, and rubbing deadened buttocks back to life. Harry slung his kit bag over his shoulder and followed the group into the building and through to a grand hall filled with rows of bunks. He gazed up at the vaulted ceiling lined with wooden beams. Quite a contrast to the utilitarian dormitory of the barracks. He and Arthur flung their bags on adjacent beds and smiled a greeting to two soldiers reclining on nearby bunks, who immediately stood up to shake hands and introduce themselves as Les and Arch.

"When did you arrive?" asked Arthur, patting his pockets for cigarettes.

"About a week ago," replied Les. Harry studied the bright-eyed young man, his face covered in freckles. Was he even eighteen?

"Apart from morning drills and vehicle maintenance, you get quite a lot of free time."

"I like the sound of that," said Arthur.

"And the locals treat you like royalty," added Arch, who appeared equally young. "The pubs aren't bad either."

Arthur looked at Harry. "Well, my friend, I think we need to go and check that out, don't you think?"

"Couldn't agree more," said Harry. "Fancy a pint, lads?"

***

They rounded up the new arrivals and with Les and Arch leading the way, the group strolled to the nearest pub. Inside was a mass of men in khaki, the air thick with smoke. The men squeezed through the crowd to the bar, where a smartly dressed landlord was pulling foaming pints in quick succession. Once served, they escaped the crush and emerged into the sunshine, squinting after the gloom of the pub. Arch nodded towards the far end of the high street.

"The main camp is up on the common. We're lucky to be billeted indoors."

Three nurses dressed in the distinctive blue uniform of the Voluntary Aid Detachment, walked by. An anonymous wolf whistle emitted from the throng causing them to blush and hurry on.

"There's a convalescence hospital just up the road," said Les, his eyes fixed on the nurses.

Arthur gave him a nudge. "You're only here for a couple of weeks, you know."

Colour rose to the young man's cheeks, and he smiled sheepishly. Arthur continued, pointing his finger like a preacher to his followers. "Remember the army's words of warning, lads. *'Never forget the dual temptations of wine and women. Fear God and do your duty'."*

Les took a final glance at the retreating nurses.

***

The three weeks Harry and Arthur spent in Hungerford turned out to be the most relaxing and enjoyable since their enlistment. They had the chance to practice driving ambulance cars, endeavouring to master the awkward gear changes and learning to manoeuvre the unfamiliar vehicles. They took advantage of the French grammar books circulating amongst the men to learn key words and phrases and they also spent a considerable amount of time in the pubs.

Ten days after arriving, they found themselves in the fields surrounding the town helping a local farmer with his haymaking. It was a glorious morning with a clear sky and no hint of a breeze. Two horses harnessed to a hay waggon, stood waiting while the sweet-smelling grass was stacked higher and higher. Harry straightened his back and wiped his sleeve across his forehead. He leant for a moment on the rake and surveyed the scene. The farmer was swinging his scythe in broad strokes, the hay collapsing at his feet like maidens swooning. The army volunteers were toiling alongside two burly farmhands, while skylarks sung high above them, invisible in the bright sky. One of the horses snorted and stamped a hoof. Harry soaked up the warm energy from both the sun and the tableau laid out before him. It felt restorative, like a tonic helping to heal a deep and painful wound.

He caught sight of the farmer's wife approaching with an enormous wicker basket, three little ones running round her skirt. She called the workers over and pulled back a checked cloth to reveal shiny pork pies and bottles of golden cider. The men gathered round and tucked into the feast. After the monotony of army rations, Harry had never tasted anything so delicious. He watched the children rolling in the hay and clambering over the farmer. The eldest broke away and approached the waiting horses, undaunted by their size. He stretched up to stroke them and they bent down to nuzzle him. Retrieving a carrot from his pocket, he broke it in half and offered it on flattened palms. One of the horses nudged him for more, sending him tumbling backwards, giggling. The boy got to his feet and started stroking the long noses, whispering soft words.

As the sun met the horizon, the group headed back to the farmhouse with tired muscles and weary limbs.

***

On a day in early September, the men were queuing outside the hospital, where a doctor was administering vaccinations for typhoid fever. The weather was bright and sunny, summer warmth persisting. With morning duties completed, the mood was light, and the men smoked and chatted in the sunshine.

Arthur opened his cigarette case and offered one to Harry who was fiddling with his collar trying to loosen the scratchy material. He undid the top button and as he rubbed his chafed neck, spotted Arch hurrying towards them with an air of excitement. He clearly had news to tell.

"We're off, lads," he said. "I overheard the CO. We go tomorrow."

There was a moment of quiet while the news sunk in, then cheering broke out. Arthur clapped Harry on the back. "Well, this is it, mate. Nervous?"

Harry shook his head. "No, mate, can't wait."

***

Early the following morning, the motor convoy paraded down the high street, cheered on by crowds of locals, and then joined the main road to Bristol and Avonmouth docks.

Chapter Seven

It was a starless night with heavy cloud cover and a gusty wind. Harry pulled the collar of his army coat up against the chill and watched England disappearing into the inky blackness. There was nothing left for him there. It wouldn't matter if he never saw those shores again. He listened to the hushed conversations around him, interrupted every so often by a burst of laughter. Everyone on board was excited and although it was a night crossing, no one was going to sleep. The boat was laden with the necessities of war. Artillery guns, supplies, soldiers, doctors, nurses, and the horses that would carry the officers and pull the canons and waggons.

Despite the sea breeze, Harry could smell cigarette smoke mixed with the unmistakable odour of animals. He had watched the horses as they were unceremoniously hoisted in large tarpaulin slings from quayside to hold, their legs dangling like marionettes. He wondered what they were making of it all. Occasionally he picked up the sound of a snort or a nervous whinny coming from somewhere below. His mind went to Mary and the worn copy of Black Beauty she used to keep by the bed. Her favourite book, read a hundred times, waiting for the next generation of reader.

"Excuse me?"

He jumped and turned to see a woman with a cigarette in her hand. She had pale skin and eyes a sapphire blue.

"Didn't mean to startle you. Do you have a light at all?"

"Yes. Yes, course."

Retrieving a small box from his coat pocket he pulled out a match. The woman leant in as he struck it and he cupped his hand around to shield it from the breeze, but the wind caught it and the flame disappeared. She smiled and waited while he tried again. The light fluttered then died once more. Laughing, she stepped back and tucked a strand of loose hair under her hat. For an instant, Harry forgot about the match. The woman cleared her throat. He quickly focussed and grabbed another. This time he managed to shelter it and the flame held just long enough for the end of the cigarette to start glowing.

"Thank you." She turned and leaned against the railings. "Wonder when we'll see England again?" she said, blowing out a long stream of smoke. Harry looked at where the coastline had finally melted into the darkness.

"Maybe never."

The woman studied him for a moment. Harry found he couldn't return her gaze and peered out into the gloom. She glanced at the soldiers, huddled in groups around the deck.

"You're not sitting with the other men," she said.

"Just having a bit of time to myself," he replied. He shot a look in her direction and ventured, "You're not sitting with the other women."

She looked over her shoulder then leant in. Harry detected the light aroma of her scent.

"I'm not supposed to be smoking. Against regulations." She flashed him a smile, revealing white, even teeth. Harry was about to respond when a voice interrupted.

"Rose, come on. There's tea and biscuits!" A blonde woman was beckoning.

"Better go. Thank you for the light." She tossed her cigarette into the sea and turned to join her friend. "Good luck," she called as she walked away. Harry's eyes followed her until she was lost from view, swallowed up by the crowd, like a bee returning to the hive.

***

A short while later, he discovered Arthur playing cards with a group of unwitting despatch riders who were slowly and surely losing their supply of cigarettes. Harry had witnessed many unsuspecting card players lose their 'fortune' over the past weeks and never ceased to be amazed by Arthur's luck. Eventually enthusiasm for the game dwindled and Arthur gathered up the cards with the usual grin. He began to pocket his winnings.

"Thank you, gentlemen. It's been a pleasure." The men drifted away, grumbling and cursing. Harry flopped down.

"I see you're making new friends."

Arthur held his hands up, "Hey, nobody forced them." He kept back two of the cigarettes, handed one to Harry and put the other between his lips. "And what have you been up to while I've been topping up our supply of smokes?"

He struck a match and Harry leant in. "Nothing. Just thinking."

Arthur studied him for a moment then held the pack of cards up. "Fancy pontoon?"

Harry snorted. "You must be joking. After what I've just witnessed?"

***

The men re-joined their group and spent the rest of the journey smoking and speculating on what lay ahead. As the first glimmer of light crept up from the east, Harry detected a change in the sound of the engines and the ship began to slow. Everyone began to stir from their uncomfortable pitches on the deck, stretching and rubbing cold limbs. The sea air was raw. Harry jogged up and down trying to get warm. He and Arthur joined the crowd lining the railings, every one of them silently hypnotized by the sight of France appearing below a watery sky.

***

The docks were buzzing. Unloading started immediately and instructions were being shouted from every direction. Guns, horses, motorcycles, and supplies all had to be carefully manoeuvred onto the quay. Harry spied a seemingly endless troop train and rows of army vehicles standing by. He was surprised to see that despite the early hour, locals had gathered to welcome the boat, waving flags, and cheering.

"Vive l'Angleterre! Vive le roi!" they called.

The infantry soldiers were the first to disembark and filed to the waiting train which would take them to the port of Etaples. Affectionately called Eat Apples by the British, the town had become the largest Allied base outside of England, due to its network of railways, roads and canals. It was now home to camps, hospitals, and transport depots. Harry had heard stories about the rigorous routine and iron discipline of the infamous training camp, nicknamed the Bull Ring.

"Poor buggers," said Arthur at his shoulder. "To think that was going to be us."

Harry watched the troops marching away, rifles on their shoulders. "Yeh, to think that was going to be us."

They collected their kit bags and followed the slow-moving queue down the gangplank and towards a waiting truck. Harry heard female voices and turned to glance into the back of an open truck. Blue eyes met his gaze and as a look of recognition flashed across the woman's face, she smiled and waved at him, prompting wide-eyed looks from the group around her. He gave a shy wave and walked on, guessing Arthur had witnessed the exchange.

"Well, well, Private Stone. You are full of surprises."

Harry ignored him and hurried on, leaving Arthur smiling to himself.

***

Two hours later, after a cramped and bumpy ride, the small convoy arrived in the town of Merville. Harry peered out at the busy streets and gazed up at the ornate brick and stone buildings with their steep roofs and decorative gables. They passed a red-brick clock tower like the one in Hungerford. It was hard to believe life seemed to be carrying on as normal when he knew the fighting was just a few miles away.

The truck left the town centre and joined a road leading out into the countryside. A few minutes later, they drove through a sturdy-looking gate into a large farmyard. The men jumped down and took in their new surroundings. Ambulances were coming and going, and mechanics were busy working under raised bonnets. There were small groups of drivers dotted round the yard, some eating, some even asleep, propped awkwardly against a wall or a vehicle wheel. They were just soldiers like him, but Harry couldn't work out why they looked different. And then it struck him. There were all filthy and every last one of them looked utterly exhausted.

Two officers emerged from the main farmhouse and the soldiers stood to attention.

"At ease, gentlemen. Hope you had a good journey. My name is Captain Bate. This is Lieutenant Kerr. You will shortly be shown to your quarters and then to the mess. I'm sure you're all ready for a brew. You will be required to orientate yourselves quickly and be operational within forty-eight hours. Make sure you familiarise yourselves with your allocated vehicle. Study the maps and talk to the other drivers." The captain nodded at the lieutenant and added, "We are sorely in need of your services, gentlemen. Welcome to the Western Front."

Chapter Eight

The day had the promise of late summer warmth, but the sun hadn't yet burnt off the low cloud. Harry stepped outside and listened to the rumbling of the guns in the distance. He was here at last. Though England seemed a million miles away, the pain had come with him. It was always going to be there.

He heard an engine revving and turned to see an ambulance reversing out of one of the workshops. The abandoned farm had been requisitioned by the Royal Army Medical Corps for No 2 Convoy the previous October. The expansive farmyard was ideal for parking thirty or so ambulance cars and two sheds were now fully equipped repair and maintenance workshops. The large farmhouse kitchen had been modified with the addition of portable stoves and a long bench for food preparation. Some trestle tables and a collection of mismatched chairs had been squeezed into two ground floor rooms forming the mess. Billets for the men had been created in the remaining rooms and an outbuilding housed a rudimentary ablution block. One of the bedrooms was now the office.

He crossed the yard and surveyed the car he had inherited from a driver on leave. What a sorry looking thing. The front and sides were splattered with mud and the windscreen was barely visible through the grime. He noticed one of the wipers was broken. As he moved round the vehicle, he glanced at the familiar red cross painted on the side. What had once been a vivid scarlet was now a dirty, rust colour. He pulled back the grubby canvas flap and peered in. There were slats for four stretchers, two sets either side, one above the other, and a roof made of narrow wooden planks. But what grabbed his attention was the blood stains. On the walls. Across the floor. Some old and others clearly much fresher. Jesus.

Arthur appeared at his side. "It's a grim sight, that's for sure," he said. "Mine's the same."

Harry continued staring at the grisly scene. What did he expect? He let the flap drop down, returned to the front, and jumped up behind the steering wheel. The cab was as dirty as the exterior. An empty can of bully beef lay on the floor, along with some discarded cigarette packets and used matches. A small area of the windscreen had been wiped to allow some visibility. Harry peeked through it and saw Arthur making his way towards him carrying two buckets of water. He put one down and called up to him. "I reckon we can give these cars a lick and a promise before breakfast, eh?"

The friends worked quickly, sluicing down the wheels and sides and scrubbing the windscreens. After a few minutes they became aware they had an audience.

"You're wasting your time, lads."

"Wouldn't bother if I were you."

"Won't stay clean for long, you know."

The hecklers were talking from experience and clearly had a point, but Harry and Arthur carried on regardless.

"Take no notice," said Arthur. "It's all about standards." He walked round to inspect Harry's handiwork. "My boss may have thought a little too much of himself, but he did teach me a lot. An immaculate uniform and a spotless motor vehicle show pride and self-respect."

Harry absorbed Arthur's words while the hecklers grew bored and wandered away. He threw one last bucket of water over the bonnet, gathered up the debris from the cab and followed Arthur into breakfast.

They queued for tea and bread and jam, then took seats opposite two privates who were sharing a joke. One introduced himself as Frank, a large, solid man with a round, friendly face. The other was slim and pale, slightly ill-looking Harry thought, but no less friendly. Frank called him Billy Billy, but Harry resisted the urge to ask why. He detected a Midlands accent.

The new arrivals were keen to hear about conditions at the Front and quizzed the two men.

"Whatever you've heard, it's ten times worse," said Frank.

Billy nodded in agreement. "It's true, it's true."

Frank continued. "When there's an offensive on, the dead and wounded just keep coming. Poor bastards." He took a loud slurp of his tea. "U.B.C."

"U.B.C?" said Harry.

"Utter bloody chaos. But they're not moving up at the moment. It's a bit of a stalemate, so it's mainly shrapnel wounds from shells. A few of the lads are getting trench fever. And every so often you'll get some poor sod who stuck his head up too high, and a sniper's got him."

Billy leant forward and whispered excitedly, "But we got a nod something's in the pipeline. A push forward, east of here. That's when it'll really kick off."

"Yeh," said Frank. "Something the French are cooking up, we heard, but Second Army is in on it. And wherever the Second Army goes, we go." He grinned. "Better prepare yourselves, lads."

Harry noticed the grin on Frank's face quickly disappear when he thought no one was looking. They were joined by a man with striking looks and a spotless uniform, who introduced himself as Joseph. As he shook hands with the newcomers, Harry couldn't help but stare at his piercing eyes and shaved head.

"Joseph is our motorcycle rider," said Frank.

"Oh really?" said Harry. "What make of bike?"

"Triumph Model H," replied Joseph, dropping down

next to him. "Do you ride?"

"No, never had the chance. I'd love to have a go though."

"Well, we'll have to try and arrange that."

They spent the remainder of breakfast discussing routes and distances to the various casualty clearing stations and stationary hospitals. According to Frank and Billy, the maps were worth looking at, but the situation changed quickly and some of them were already out of date.

Half an hour later the men wiped their plates clean and drained the last of their tea. As they emerged into the yard, they heard engines approaching and all eyes turned to the farm gate. Three ambulances trundled in and parked alongside the other cars. One of the drivers was a tall soldier with blonde hair and a slim moustache. He leapt down from his cab, flung his cap on the seat and bellowed, "Jones. Where the hell are you?"

A mechanic nervously appeared from out of a workshop, wiping his hands on a dirty rag. The driver strode towards him, red in the face and shouting as he approached. "You're a bloody useless excuse for a mechanic, Jones. Third gear went again."

The man was visibly shaking by this point and had taken a few steps back as the furious driver advanced. Frank turned to Harry and Arthur, "That, gentlemen, is Edward Carter. Heir to a small fortune, self-confessed ladies' man and complete arse."

The men chuckled at Frank's description. "And the object of his anger is Seth Jones, one of the best mechanics in the army."

As Carter reached Seth, he gave him a hard shove in the chest, sending the mechanic stumbling backwards. Harry bristled.

"Problem is," continued Frank, "Carter's uncle is a

Major General, making him more or less untouchable. And doesn't he know it?"

"Poor Seth. Poor Seth," murmured Billy.

As the men dispersed, Carter cast an angry look across at them and noticed Harry staring. He gave him a withering look and turned his attention back to the unfortunate mechanic.

***

Edward Carter had been a source of continual disappointment to his parents. The family had made their money in the tea plantations of India, until the third generation decided to break the cycle and pursue careers in the military. Edward's father, Sydney and uncle, Thomas, sailed through officer training and rose quickly up the ranks. The brothers fought side by side in the Boar War, but whilst Thomas continued on a star-studded path, Sydney returned with life-changing injuries and was promptly invalided out of the army he so loved. He made plans for his only son to follow in his footsteps and, once he was of age, enter the hallowed portals of Sandhurst.

Edward had been educated at Cranleigh but despite the highest standards of teaching, he had struggled with the academic side as well as the discipline of boarding school. To his father's dismay, he completed his education with few qualifications and none of the requirements for entering the military academy. Edward himself felt nothing but relief.

When one of the housemaids fell pregnant, having been unable to fend off a drunken Edward, Sydney was eager to avoid a scandal. He paid off the young woman and installed his son in an apartment in Mayfair, from where Edward revelled in all the pleasures London had to offer.

It was only when another war loomed and there was a call to arms that Sydney realised his dreams of living vicariously through his son were not necessarily over. Edward, however, had other plans. With no desire to carry a rifle and terrified of facing the enemy, he ordered his father's chauffeur to instruct him in driving the family automobile. It seemed Sydney's dreams of a fighting son were to be dashed after all.

***

The newcomers were led through the morning routine. Checking fuel levels. Examining the wheels to ensure the solid rubber tyres were sound. Double-checking with the mechanics that any repair work had been carried out. They were to be paired with an experienced driver and ride as passenger for the day. It was an opportunity to familiarise themselves with the geography of the area and experience the evacuation chain for the first time.

Harry was teamed up with a driver called Dev Arya, a young man with jet black hair, and large, brown eyes. He had an air of eagerness which Harry was instantly drawn to. The convoy had been ordered to transport casualties from an advanced dressing station six miles northeast of headquarters to No. 7 Casualty Clearing Station on the outskirts of Merville.

The roads were muddy and congested with troops and vehicles and the ambulance bumped and bounced along. Dev expertly negotiated the deep ruts and carefully manoeuvred around supply waggons and horses.

"How long have you been in France?" asked Harry, almost hitting his head as a large bump in the road lifted him out of his seat.

"Arrived last October, so nearly a year," replied Dev, dropping a gear as the car struggled up a small incline. "Just in time for the battle at Ypres. It was a baptism of fire."

"You must have enlisted right at the beginning of the war, then?" said Harry.

"Yep. Me and my best mate, William. We signed up together. We were so excited…"

His voice trailed off and he looked away. Harry wasn't sure what to say, but then Dev continued, "We were both stable boys, so they had us driving horse-drawn ambulances at first. Never worked so hard in my life!" He paused, lost in the memory for a moment.

"Anyway, then the motor ambulances came along, and the army taught us to drive."

Harry waited, sensing Dev had more to say.

"The Germans shelled William's convoy back in the spring. No survivors."

Harry had no idea what words of comfort he could offer this man he'd only just met. At that moment Dev swerved violently to avoid a pothole and Harry grabbed the seat to stop himself from falling out of the cab, his alarm bringing a smile to Dev's face.

***

As they neared the front line, the sound of explosions grew louder. Harry felt the ground shake and looked across at Dev, who didn't seem to have noticed. They passed a large crater occupied by a crowd of bedraggled soldiers sitting smoking. Despite their obvious exhaustion, the group were talking and laughing. Harry spotted a small terrier wandering amongst the men, happily receiving a stroke here and a pat there.

Ten minutes later they pulled up at the dressing station where activity was frantic. Dev pulled on the handbrake. "This doesn't look good," he said.

"What's happening?" asked Harry, jumping in his seat as a shell landed just yards away.

"Looks like they're evacuating."

Stretcher bearers were ready and waiting and loaded up with an increasing sense of urgency. "I'd get out of here as soon as possible," urged one of them. "We're abandoning the station. The Jerries are too close."

Another explosion ripped up the ground nearby. Harry could feel his heart thumping in his chest and his throat was dry. The air was thick with tension. Casualties on board, he and Dev leapt into the cab and prepared to depart, but the driver in front was struggling to start his car.

"Come on, come on," said Dev, tapping the steering wheel. A long minute later, the vehicle lurched forward and moved off.

"Right, let's go," said Dev.

In that moment, everything Harry could see exploded in a mass of metal and earth and a deafening boom filled his ears. He and Dev ducked down as shrapnel showered down on the car, cracking the windscreen. As the air cleared, they slowly sat up and peered through the damaged glass. A shell had landed directly on the ambulance in front of them. It was now a twisted wreck, unrecognisable as a vehicle. Harry stared in horror. He became aware of a voice shouting and realised an officer was yelling at them to leave.

"Go! Go now!"

Dev slammed the car into gear, manoeuvred around the smoking wreckage and accelerated away. Harry stared ahead in silence, trying to take in what he'd witnessed. So driving ambulances wasn't the breeze he'd thought it was going to be.

"You alright?" asked Dev.

He took a breath. "Yeh, yeh, I'm fine." He glanced

sideways. "Did you know that driver?"

"I've seen him before, but he's not…he wasn't from No 2 convoy. Poor chap. Bloody rotten luck."

Harry returned his eyes to the road ahead. "Yes. Bloody rotten luck."

***

An hour later, the road led them briefly through a wooded area and then out into open fields where the Casualty Clearing Station lay before them. Harry was stunned.

"My God," he said. There was row upon row of white tents stretching endlessly across the green expanse. He could see figures moving in between the neat rows and in and out of the tents. Ambulance cars were coming and going.

"Impressive, eh?" said Dev. "They've got wards, theatres, x-ray, mess halls and billets."

"Can't believe the size of it," said Harry.

Drop-off was well organised and swift. Orderlies expertly unloaded the stretchers whilst a medical officer issued directions. Within minutes the casualties had been whisked away and Harry and Dev were back on the move again. Harry ventured to ask about Dev's family.

"My father works for the same family I was a stable boy for. Rich landowners in Surrey. Nice people. Pa is a sort of gardener come groundsman. That's where he met my mother. The family spends winters in India. My mother was a maid for them and one day they asked if she wanted to work for them back in England. She jumped at the chance apparently. And as soon as my father set eyes on her, it was love at first sight. A couple of years later they had my sister and then yours truly came along." He grinned, revealing the whitest teeth Harry had ever seen.

They returned to headquarters tired and hungry. At supper, Harry took a seat next to Arthur and asked him about his day, motioning to Dev to join them. Dev was laughing at a joke and looking over his shoulder when he bumped straight into Carter, sending tea slopping down Carter's tunic.

"What the hell are you doing?"

"Sorry, Carter," said Dev, stepping back. The room went quiet. Carter looked Dev up and down and said, "Shouldn't you be with your own kind, picking tea leaves somewhere?"

Harry rose from the bench and Carter clocked him out of the corner of his eye, but his attention was still on Dev, and he now had an audience. "And where's your turban by the way?"

Dev stepped towards him. "I'm not a Sikh. I'm Hindu."

"It's all the same thing."

Harry made a movement, but Dev raised the palm of his hand and shook his head. Carter snorted and gave Dev a shove in the chest. "Watch where you're going next time."

Conversation resumed.

"You should have let me lamp him," said Harry.

"Thanks, but I have my own way of dealing with people like him," said Dev.

***

Over the following two weeks, Harry and the other newcomers settled into the convoy's routine. A steady stream of casualties from the frontline meant continuous runs to and from the dressing stations. Some days they unloaded at a clearing station, other days at a hospital barge or an ambulance train. Harry quickly learnt to handle the cumbersome car on the rutted roads, getting to grips with the grinding gears and heavy steering. And gradually, he began to feel part of the team.

***

One evening in the last week of September, the men were called to assemble in the yard. As they gathered, Billy came up to Harry and whispered in his ear, "It's the news we've been waiting for."

A serious-looking Captain Bate stood before them.

"At ease, gentlemen." He ran his finger around his shirt collar. "In the early hours of tomorrow morning, Second Army, along with French forces, will be launching an offensive in the town of Loos, six miles east of Merville. An advanced dressing station will be established on Rue des Lostes, west of Loos and No. 2 Convoy is ordered to attend. The main dressing station will be in La Gorgue. Cases going to a casualty clearing station will be taken to No. 7. Departure 0800 hours. Get some sleep. We've a rough couple of weeks ahead of us."

Harry glanced over at Arthur, who gave him a grim smile. Billy came up and said excitedly, "I was right. I was right."

Harry couldn't tell if Billy's exuberance was due to the imminent battle or the fact his information had been correct. He looked across at Frank, who had lit a cigarette and was staring into the distance. As he walked over, he noticed him quickly switch to his usual happy face.

"Well, your first battle then, eh?" he said, offering Harry a cigarette. Harry leant into the match Frank had struck.

"How're you feeling?" asked Frank.

"Alright, I think," replied Harry, removing a piece of tobacco from his mouth. "More of what we've been doing, I suppose. Just in larger numbers."

"Yeh. Larger numbers." Frank took a long drag on his cigarette and turned his head in the direction of the Front. A break in the shellfire had created an eerie silence.

"Those poor sods," he said, shaking his head. "But we've got to stick it to old Fritz, haven't we?"

"That we do."

***

The following morning was damp and foggy. The men were up early though few of them had the stomach for the hot breakfast the cook had prepared especially.

"Eat while you have the chance," said Frank, as he watched Harry nudge his food around the plate. "Force it down, lad."

Half an hour later, the drivers were in their cars, engines running. Harry's palms were damp with sweat and slippery on the steering wheel. He wiped them on his tunic as he watched the lead ambulance crawl out of the gate. Arthur followed and gave him a reassuring nod as he passed. He crunched the long lever into first gear and joined the snaking convoy as it trundled slowly towards the Front.

Chapter Nine

The soldier let out a scream as he writhed on the stretcher. One of the bearers leant over him.

"It's alright, lad. You're off to Blighty now."

He was carefully lifted up into the ambulance whilst Harry picked up his helmet from where it had fallen and placed it on top of the blanket. A long row of casualties lay side by side along the road. Some of them moaning or crying, some ominously quiet. Harry could see the straw scattered beneath them, was already stained a deep red. The injured who had been able to make their own way to the dressing station were sitting wrapped in blankets with a mug of tea in one hand and a cigarette or a slice of bread in the other.

A shell exploded beyond a wood just half a mile away. Harry listened to the boom of artillery and crack of gunfire coming from the east. He felt the ground shake and noticed dust and mortar falling away from the crumbling wall of the farmhouse. Some houses in the area were still occupied, the residents undeterred by the advancing Germans and eager to offer food and shelter to the Allies. This farm, however, appeared to have been abandoned many months ago, possibly at the beginning of the war when the Kaiser's army was sweeping through Belgium and into northern France. Last year's harvest of hay was sitting rotting in an open-sided barn and some children's toys lay dotted around the yard, discarded in the rushed departure. One of the orderlies had told him they'd found a dying dog under a cart in the barn, left to fend for itself in the panic of fleeing an approaching enemy. Where was the family now?

He turned to see his car was full, the sixth load that day. One of the stretcher bearers leant towards him. "The lad with the stomach wound's not looking too good. Put your foot down if you can."

Harry jumped up into his cab and waited as a small convoy approached. He tried to see if Arthur was amongst them. He hadn't seen him for several hours. He didn't spot Arthur, but he did get a thumbs up from Frank as he drove by, his large frame filling the cab.

It was slow progress over the muddy roads, and he had to work hard to avoid the deep ruts. Wrestling with the gears, the wheels spun in the mire. The words of the bearer kept playing in his head but every time he sped up, the thin rubber tyres hit a rut and a cry came from the back. He winced. "Sorry, lads."

But if he slowed down too much, he risked getting stuck. By the time he joined the queue of cars at the dressing station his tunic was damp with sweat and his neck and shoulders ached. He stepped down from the cab as two orderlies rushed up and flung back the canvas. One of the casualties had raised himself up on one elbow. He looked at them and shook his head. "He went quiet ten minutes ago," he said.

Harry helped to unload, tossing helmets to one side, and piling the stained blankets at his feet, ready to be used on the next run. Whilst he waited for the orderlies to return, he climbed into the back of the car and crouched down next to the young soldier. Christ. He couldn't have been much more than eighteen. With a sickening lurch of his stomach, he suddenly recognised the lifeless face and for a moment he was back at his window watching his neighbours bid farewell to their son. He turned over the medical card, attached to a tunic button by a length of string. John Garbutt. Private. 11th Division, K1 Army. Gunshot wound to the stomach. What a bloody waste. All that vitality and enthusiasm gone. Another child paying the ultimate price for his country. Another family destroyed for ever. He gently pulled the blanket over the boy's face.

***

It was nightfall when he pulled into the yard and switched off his engine. He sat in the gloom, unable to move, the images of the day flashing before him. A kaleidoscope of bandages, blood, and bodies. Aware of someone approaching, he turned to see Arthur standing by the cab, his face pale and drawn and his tunic dirty and smeared with blood.

"You seem to be in need of a wash, Private," said Harry.

Arthur smiled and replied, "Most definitely. But first things first."

"Game of cards?"

"Grub."

***

The drivers were up early the next morning, ready for a repeat of the previous day. As they gathered in the yard, Harry watched Joseph preparing to depart, a knapsack hanging at each hip, their straps forming an 'x' across his chest. He adjusted his armbands and fixed his goggles over his eyes. The motorcycle spluttered into life, and he gave the group a wave as he accelerated out of the gate. Captain Bate appeared.

"Right men, the good news is, despite our boys being hampered by the early morning fog, the enemy line east of Loos was successfully breached."

A cheer went up.

"The Allies are making another push today so expect high numbers of casualties. Unfortunately, we're also going to see cases of gas poisoning. By all accounts the wind blew some of it back into our own trenches. They're going to start feeling symptoms today." The captain looked up at the threatening clouds and added, "The weather is closing in. Grab some breakfast. Departure at 0730 hours."

***

Breakfast eaten, Harry emerged from the farm building as giant raindrops began to bounce off the yard and vehicles. Perfect. More mud. He turned up his collar and dashed across to the workshops, hoping to have a quick word with one of the mechanics. He knew they'd been working through the night to ensure the cars were fit for another gruelling day on the water-logged roads. As he pulled back the heavy wooden door, the smell of oil, grease and petrol hit him. A pair of legs was protruding from under an ambulance and Harry gave them a nudge with his foot.

"Morning, Seth."

A grimy face appeared. "How d'you know it was me?"

"I'd know those legs anywhere!"

"'Ere, less of that. Cheeky bugger." Seth stood up and rubbed the back of his arm across his forehead. His eyes were sunken with dark circles under them, but he managed a smile.

"And what can I do for you this fine morning?" he asked.

Harry was just about to reply when a loud voice roared from the yard.

"Jones."

A look of panic flashed across the mechanic's face. "Surely not," he said.

The workshop door flew open, and Carter stormed in. Harry stepped towards him.

"Out the way, Stone," said Carter.

"Seth is dealing with me at the moment, Carter. Come back later."

Carter's face started to darken. "You know damn well I can't come back later. We're heading out. He still hasn't fixed my gears, the halfwit. Now get out the way."

Harry heard Seth behind him quietly mutter he'd done them during the night and gave a little laugh.

"What's so funny?" Carter's face twisted with rage.

"Nothing." Harry smiled broadly. "But could you leave now please. I'm sure Seth has everything sorted."

Carter looked as though he was about to explode. He took a step forward and squared up to Harry, but Harry's patience had run out and he leant into Carter's face.

"Look, Carter. I've asked politely. Twice. Now piss off or you'll find my fist down your throat." He braced himself, prepared for a fight. But Carter shrivelled like a burst balloon. His shoulders dropped and he stumbled back, glaring at the two men in turn then retreating out of the door. Harry spun round, beaming, but the mechanic looked serious.

"Thanks, Harry. But I think you might have just made an enemy there."

"I can handle men like Carter," said Harry, but a part of him thought Seth was probably right.

***

He was on his fourth run and the rain was still falling steadily. The roads were no more than quagmires and each circuit seemed to take twice as long as the last. Progress was hampered by heavy congestion as men and supplies were being moved up the line. He pulled over time and again to allow troops to pass, watching them march on to heaven knows what. Stick it to them, lads.

A short time later he pulled up alongside Billy, who was loaded up and ready to leave. Harry hopped down and called over,

"How's it going, Billy?"

"Not bad. Not bad. Seen Frank at all?"

"Not since we left HQ."

"Right, right . Better go." Billy jumped in his cab and pulled away, the wheels spinning and sliding. Two bearers approached Harry's ambulance carrying a casualty with a capital M marked on his forehead. Morphine administered. The soldier was semi-conscious and muttering incoherently.

"Main dressing station for this lot," said one of the men.

Harry flung a blanket over the moaning figure. More stretchers arrived. He climbed into the cab and started the engine. As he pressed the accelerator the wheels immediately started to spin. Come on, girl. He grimaced and gently put pressure on the pedal again. The back end suddenly swung to the left with a jolt. A cry came from the back. He put the car in reverse. He felt the wheels grip and the vehicle slowly moved backwards. He crunched it into first and the ambulance freed itself. With a sigh of relief, he called out, "We're off, lads," not expecting a reply.

**

As the runs continued, Harry lost track of time. It must have been afternoon when an orderly at one of the dressing stations offered him a mug of steaming soup. He could not have been more grateful and quickly devoured the hot, savoury broth, realising he hadn't eaten for hours. He was just taking the last drag of a cigarette when he felt a tap on his shoulder. He turned to see Joseph removing his hat and gloves. His face was grimy and mud-splattered except for large white circles around his eyes where his goggles had been sitting.

"Got a spare smoke?" he asked, wiping his sleeve across his face.

Harry dug out a crumpled packet from his breast pocket and handed it over.

"Where're you heading?"

"Back to HQ," replied Joseph, pulling out a cigarette. "The motorcycle's playing up. Been bogged down half a dozen times already."

"This rain's a sod," said Harry, flicking the stub away.

"Just hope I make it back."

Suddenly the sound of jeering erupted, and everyone turned their heads. Marching up the road, under heavy guard, was a group of German prisoners. Taunts and jibes were being thrown at them as they passed. Even some of the wounded on stretchers were joining in. Harry was transfixed. His first sight of the enemy. Anonymous up until now. Unseen. They were filthy with gaunt faces and were trudging rather than marching. A gruff voice beside him broke Harry's trance.

"Heard about this lot."

"What do you mean?" asked Harry, his eyes still following the procession.

"The clearing parties found them hiding in the village."

He turned his head towards the owner of the voice. It was one of the walking wounded, his arm in a sling and a cigarette dangling from his lips. He gave a cough then continued.

"They've left the houses in a right state apparently, especially the kitchens. Peeing on everything, and worse. So's we can't use them. Dirty bastards."

Harry watched the last of the prisoners pass by. The

spectacle disappeared round the corner and there was a flurry of activity as everyone went back to work. He realised Joseph had left without saying goodbye.

***

The final run of the day was to a clearing station in Merville. The rain had finally eased but night was falling, bringing an autumn chill. He was tired beyond belief and ravenously hungry. He rubbed his neck then dropped out of the cab. Nurses and orderlies were dashing from tent to tent. He wearily gathered up the soiled blankets and flung them in the back of the car then leant against the vehicle to rest his eyes for a moment.

"Are you alright, Private?"

Harry looked up and found himself peering straight into a pair of startling blue eyes.

Chapter Ten

Rose smoothed down her apron and adjusted her cuffs. She checked her white cotton cap in the cracked mirror propped up on the tallboy, tucking some stray hairs out of sight. The Senior Sister was a stickler for an immaculate uniform. Not that Rose blamed her. She planned to be equally exacting when she was in charge. Amy was only just putting on her apron with her hair still to do. Always running late. Rose took a deep breath.

"Here, I'll help you," she said.

"Thanks," replied Amy, rubbing at a smudge she'd spotted on her sleeve. "Oh no. Look at this. Sister Brown'll go mad." She grabbed a small handkerchief from the bedside table, quickly licked it and continued rubbing at the mark.

"We're going to be late, Amy."

"I know. Sorry. You go ahead."

"No, no. I think it's better if we arrive together. I'll do your hair."

Rose worked as swiftly as she could with Amy's mass of unruly curls and managed to tame them into a neat bun. She pinned on the cap while Amy pushed her feet into a pair of black ankle boots. They each wrapped a short, scarlet cape around their shoulders and hastened down the stairs into the street.

***

Their quarters were in a former convent, situated in a quiet street near the Church of Saint-Denis. Rose loved the tall, ornate buildings and quaint streets of Saint Omer. So different from London. No.10 Stationary Hospital was half a mile away and the women hurried along the busy footpaths, dodging pedestrians as best they could. At one point they both became entangled in the leads of two small, fluffy terriers. The owner was a rotund lady who raised her arms in alarm.

"*Faites attention!*" she shrieked.

"*Désolée, Madame.*" The women apologised and rushed on, giggling. The town was swarming with open-top touring cars, their uniformed passengers being rushed here and there on important army business, like insects in a busy nest. The women arrived at the hospital with moments to spare. It was an imposing, three-storey structure previously home to a catholic boarding school. Despite one wing being in a state of complete disrepair, the Royal Army Medical Corps had deemed the rest of the building ideal, with a large kitchen, plenty of office space and rooms suitable for conversion to operating theatres. The chapel next door had also been requisitioned and was now a well-ordered ward where Rose and Amy spent most of their time when on duty.

The nurses entered the ward to see the formidable Senior Sister Brown briefing the new shift. She gave them a fierce look as they sidled up. "You're late."

"Sorry, Sister," they said in unison.

The other nurses cast Rose and Amy sympathetic glances. The briefing concluded and they began the familiar routine of bathing the patients and changing dressings. The chapel walls were lined with neatly made bunks and a further row was arranged down the middle. Only half were occupied that morning, as an ambulance train had left for the coast the previous day, leaving only the patients too sick to withstand the journey home. England already felt a million miles away to Rose. She looked up at the impressive stained-glass windows. Through them, the morning sunshine was throwing a rainbow of lights onto each bed. She knew many of the injured soldiers took comfort from the images depicted in the windows and though, much to her parent's displeasure, she had chosen not to follow a faith, she was happy her patients found some solace there.

***

She joined the other nurses who were collecting basins of warm water. Bathing the patients was a task many new nurses struggled with, feeling embarrassed and awkward. But they soon learned to complete it briskly and efficiently and put the patient at ease. She approached a bunk on the far side of the ward.

"Good morning, Private Fletcher. How are you feeling?"

"Robert. How many times, Nurse? Please call me Robert." Rose smiled at the friendly face looking up at her. She bent forward and whispered, "Alright, Robert. But only when Sister Brown's not in earshot."

The soldier winked at her. "Deal."

Rose worked swiftly but gently. The blanket covering Robert lay ominously flat where his left leg should have been. The surgeon had thought the leg could be saved, but gangrene had set in and there had been no option but to amputate. Robert had been stoic and never lost his sense of humour, only crying when ghost pains made him sweat and writhe. Rose would sit holding his hand and dab his face with a damp flannel.

She picked up the basin and said quietly, "Right, Robert. Cup of tea?"

"Got anything stronger?" he asked with a twinkle in his eye. Rose feigned a look of shock.

"At this time of the morning! Really, Private Fletcher."

"Tea it is then," he shrugged.

Rose had wanted to be a nurse for as long as she could remember. She would spend hours wrapping bandages round her toys and whispering words of comfort. A teddy with a poorly head. A doll with a broken arm. As she grew up, Florence Nightingale had become her heroine and she dreamt of making her mark on the world in a similar way. She remembered, at the age of nine, reading with fascination about the formation of Queen Alexandra's Imperial Military Nursing Service, now the official nursing branch of the British Army. She had no doubt that was the only path for her, though she knew her parents would oppose it. They were conservative and traditionalist. Her father, Charles, worked for a bank in the city whilst her mother, Eleanor, cared for and doted on her family. They lived in a modest, but comfortable, house just off the High Holborn end of Kingsway, an area not long redeveloped as part of the slum clearance. The family had moved there when Rose was twelve, following a long-awaited promotion for her father. She had enjoyed a happy childhood with her elder sister, Catherine, but as she approached adulthood, her frustrations with her parents, and their expectations of her, grew. Catherine had followed the traditional route mapped out for young ladies. Marriage and children. She had been happy to conform and excited to choose from the stream of suitors that flowed through the house. Rose loved her sister dearly, and was pleased to be her bridesmaid, but as she followed her down the aisle on her wedding day, she knew she wanted something different. Something more. A husband and a family one day, but not yet, and not someone scrutinised and approved by her parents beforehand. She yearned to escape the suffocating attentions of her mother, focussed entirely on her, now

Catherine had flown the nest.

Rose was not going to give up her dream, but she needed both her father's blessing and his financial support to be able to attend nursing college. It was going to require a well-timed discussion and a convincing argument. She determined one Sunday over lunch would be her best chance. She would accompany her parents to church, happily and willingly for a change and she would do her best to smile at the vicar as he held her hand just a little too tightly for a little too long. As expected, her mother was outraged.

"Rosamond, what an absurd idea!"

Rose bristled at the use of Rosamond but realised this was not the time to resume that particular argument.

"Charles, tell her," said her mother.

Rose detected a moment's hesitation before her father spoke. Could there be a glimmer of hope? He carefully laid his knife and fork down.

"Rosamond, your mother's right. It isn't something a young lady with your upbringing does."

She was prepared. She was hoping to exploit her father's sense of patriotism. "But remember what Uncle Stanley said?"

Charles' brother had fought in the Boer War and talked often of the impressive work the nurses had carried out in the terrible conditions. "If another war breaks out somewhere in the Empire, nurses will be needed again," she continued.

Charles glanced across at his wife, but her eyes were blazing. "Your mother and I will discuss it."

The remainder of lunch was eaten in an uneasy silence, all the while her mother's rage an angry force pervading the meal.

That night, she lay in bed listening to the raised voices coming from her parent's room. They rarely had disagreements and she felt guilty that she had caused this one. But the fact they were arguing surely meant her father was at least considering the idea? Charles left early for work the next morning, leaving Rose to spend the day avoiding her mother and her icy stares. She was sitting reading by the fire in the kitchen, when her father came in and leant against the dresser. Her heart started thumping in her chest.

"Where would you train?" he asked.

"St Bartholomew's. If they accept me," she replied, barely able to breathe.

Her father nodded. "Alright, Rosamond. But if you're serious about this, I want to see complete dedication and I want to see you at the top of the class."

She flew out of her seat and hugged him tightly. "Yes. Yes. Thank you, Father. Thank you." She suddenly stepped back. "But what about Mother?"

Her father winked at her, something Rose had never witnessed in her life. "Don't worry about your mother."

Rose was accepted into the Nursing School at St Bartholomew's Medical College, just a half hour walk from home. The new intake of students included a vivacious girl called Amy, who, it was rumoured, came from a wealthy Yorkshire family with royal connections. Rose was mesmerised by Amy from the outset. She marvelled at her relaxed attitude to all aspects of life. Timekeeping. Appearance. Acceptable levels of behaviour for women. But Amy studied hard and charmed her tutors and fellow students alike. Within days, the two women were firm friends. They completed the three-year training and gained permanent positions at St Bartholomew's. Their dedication and commitment led swiftly to promotion and as they both took on the rank of Sister, talk of war had begun to circulate. The women speculated about leaving England. And so it was, in

September 1915, the two friends set off for France with the hope of excitement and adventure.

***

Rose held the large, metal pot with both hands and poured the chestnut-coloured tea into a row of cups. She carried them carefully through to the ward and distributed them to the ever-grateful patients. The morning passed quickly as dressings were changed and beds were tidied. Major Reid, one of the surgeons, visited the ward and spoke briefly to the patients, Sister Brown attentively at his side. The nurses stood silently in a row, trying not to laugh when the soldiers pulled a face behind her back.

Shortly after, Rose was making her way to the kitchen when she realised Brown and the Major were in a hushed conversation in the hallway. She hesitated.

"We're going to be inundated. But remember, this is sensitive information. Do what you can to prepare, ensure stock cupboards are full, but refrain from telling the nurses for now. It's only a matter of days away."

***

Rose was eager to share what she'd overheard with Amy, but frustratingly the opportunity didn't arise until suppertime that evening. She waited for the other nurses at her table to finish their meal and leave. Amy was tucking into her second helping of sponge pudding. Where such a small person put all that food, Rose could never fathom. She leant forward and whispered, "Something big's about to happen."

"What do you mean?" asked Amy, through a mouthful of custard.

"A big push."

69

Amy stopped, her spoon in mid-air. "How d'you know?"

"I heard Major Reid telling Sister."

"Blimey. Did he say when?"

"Soon. In a few days."

"Maybe this'll help to end the war?" Amy said, popping the spoon in her mouth.

***

Confirmation of the plans came forty-eight hours later. All leave was cancelled, and preparations began in earnest for the influx of casualties. Rose and Amy were coming to the end of a tiring shift when a nurse approached and told them to report to Matron's office. Rose sighed and turned to Amy. "What have you done now?"

Amy held up her hands. "Nothing! I promise."

Matron was a dark-haired, petite woman in her forties. She ran a tight ship but was neither harsh nor unfair and had earned the respect of the nurses and medical officers alike. The women stood to attention in front of her desk, at a loss as to why they were there.

"Right, Sister Davidson, Sister Turner. Despite some tardiness and the occasional issue with uniform," she looked straight at Amy, who had the grace to look sheepish. "In the relatively short time you have been here, Senior Sister Brown informs me you have proved to be excellent nurses."

The women were stunned at the unexpected compliment. Matron cleared her throat and continued. "You have been assigned to the ambulance train running between Saint Omer and Merville for the duration of this offensive."

Rose and Amy were speechless.

"You will assist Senior Sister Burton. She's two nurses down due to this wretched stomach flu. Pack your belongings and report to the station tomorrow at midday. Don't let me down, ladies." And with that they were dismissed.

The friends quietly closed the door behind them. They gave each other a hug, trying not to squeal with excitement.

***

Standing in front of Saint Omer station, Rose gazed up at the three enormous glass windows and the clock face set in decorative stonework above the centre window. What were the next few weeks going to bring? She felt a tug on her sleeve. "Come on. We're going to be late," said Amy, grabbing her hand.

"Well, that's a first from you," said Rose.

The station was teeming with military personnel and the women had to forge their way through the crowds as they searched for their train. Unable to make sense of the departure board, they sought help from a harassed-looking railway official. He gave them some garbled directions in French and pointed vaguely towards a distant platform. Amy responded by giving him her sweetest smile and thanking him in purest French. They left him staring after them open-mouthed.

Their train was indeed at the furthest platform. As they approached the khaki-coloured carriages, Rose felt her stomach turn in a rush of excitement. They spotted a nurse standing beside an open door talking to a station guard. She looked round and greeted them with a smile.

"Good morning, ladies. Davidson and Turner, I presume?"

"Yes, Sister," replied Rose. "I'm Rose Davidson and

this is Amy Turner."

"I'm Senior Sister Burton. Right, let's get you settled in." She leant forward and relieved Rose of her bag. "I'll help you with that. Follow me, ladies."

Rose and Amy warmed to her immediately. They clambered up and followed her along the train. The carriages were lined with narrow, metal bunks, stacked three high, each one neatly made with two pristine white pillows at the head and a blanket folded at the foot. A hospital on rails. The Sister stopped outside a small cabin containing two narrow beds and a single shelf. She placed Rose's case on the floor and stepped out of the way.

"This is you, ladies. I'll let you unpack and then come along to the mess car, and I'll introduce you to everyone. We're due to depart in half an hour. Can't tell you how pleased I am to have you here. Oh, and the WC is at the far end of the carriage."

With that, she disappeared down the corridor and through the doors. The women quickly squeezed their belongings on the shelf, checked themselves in the cracked mirror they discovered hanging on the back of the door and made their way along the train. They entered a carriage where a group of men and women were seated around two circular tables enjoying what looked like thick soup and bread. Sister Burton stood up as Rose and Amy entered and beckoned them forward.

"Right, introductions everyone."

The chatter halted and the group turned to welcome the newcomers.

"This is Sister Davidson and Sister Turner." Rose and Amy smiled a greeting.

"And these are our Medical Officers, Major Colton and Major Fitzpatrick."

The men rose from their seats.

"How do you do," said Colton, a tall, thin man with

the largest moustache Rose had ever seen.

"Welcome aboard," said Fitzpatrick, wiping his mouth with his napkin.

"Nice to meet you, Sir," said Rose.

"And these are Sisters Green, Hawkins, Ingles and Long."

The women gave a communal 'hello' and Sister Burton gestured to Rose and Amy to sit down. Everyone resumed their lunch and conversation picked up again, this time including the new arrivals. A couple of minutes later two bowls of steaming soup were placed in front of them and Rose and Amy happily tucked in. By the time the train began to creep out of the station, they no longer felt like newcomers at all.

The journey was slow, punctuated by sudden braking, which sent supplies and belongings sliding off shelves and racks, and it was past midnight when the train crawled into Merville station. As the double-door in the centre of the carriage swung open, Rose gasped at the sight before her. She had never seen anything like it. The platform was a carpet of stretchers. Row after row of soldiers with bandaged heads, arms and legs. Stretcher bearers were picking their way through the mass of bodies. The air was filled with the sound of shouting, talking and crying and the haze of cigarette smoke was failing to mask the acrid smell of blood and unwashed bodies. A medical officer approached, tiptoeing between the stretchers. His khakis were dirty and stained and the dark circles under his eyes spoke of sleep loss and heavy workload. He gave Rose a weary greeting. "The clearing stations are full. This lot are direct from the dressing stations."

The two Majors appeared along with Sister Burton, and Rose moved aside to let them disembark. Amy was behind them, and she stared wide-eyed at the scene in front of her. The officer wished them luck and disappeared along the platform. Major Fitzpatrick turned to the nurses. "Right, fine ladies, it seems we have our work cut out so let's get to it."

***

The loading process was long and painstaking, each patient checked on to the train and treatment prescribed. Casualties with tourniquets and gangrene were marked urgent with blue pencil on their bandages. Cases of measles, mumps and scarlet fever went straight to the Infectious Carriage. The bearers manoeuvred each stretcher on board for hour after hour. Soldier after soldier.

It was after four o'clock in the morning by the time the train was ready to depart. Treatment had already begun, and the team slowly worked its way through the carriages. The French orderlies toiled alongside them, washing filthy hands and faces, removing uniforms too tattered or mud-caked to be of any more use and replacing them with fresh, clean pyjamas. They brought basin after basin of hot water and brewed gallons of tea. Rose felt the familiar mix of exhilaration and dismay. These poor boys. So resilient and brave. Never a grumble, just gratitude and a smile. She finished securing the bandage on a young private who had lost both eyes.

"That's grand," he said, giving Rose's hand a quick squeeze as he lay back on the bunk. She moved on to a sergeant with a head wound, swiftly treating the torn flesh and applying a clean bandage. She picked up the basin and offered the soldier a tot of rum.

"That's absolutely glorious," he said, "but that leg is a beast."

Rose put the basin back down on the bunk. "You have

a leg injury too?" she asked, pulling back the blanket. She tried to conceal her horror when she saw what was clearly a fractured femur. She was dumbfounded. "Oh, my goodness, why didn't you tell the medical officer?"

"Didn't want to be a bother," he replied.

Rose shook her head in disbelief. "I'll get this looked at as quickly as possible," she promised.

"Don't forget the rum," reminded the sergeant.

***

For two days the train shunted between Saint Omer and Merville. It was during an extended delay at the clearing station that Rose found herself walking past a driver leaning against his ambulance and even with his eyes closed she recognised the soldier from the boat.

Chapter Eleven

Harry stared at the nurse, temporarily at a loss for words. She looked different in the grey uniform. "Yes. Yes. I'm fine, thank you," he eventually replied, remembering to remove his cap.

"I thought it was you." She smiled warmly. "The soldier with the matches."

He laughed self-consciously.

"You look like you've had a tough day," she continued, scanning his grubby face and tunic.

"Oh, all in a day's work, you know," he said.

"I'm Rose." She held out her hand.

He wiped his dirty hand on his trousers and stepped forward. "Harry. Are you stationed here now?"

"No. I'm based at a hospital in Saint Omer, but while this offensive is on, I'm working on one of the ambulance trains. You look like you could do with a cup of tea?"

Harry hesitated, an image of Mary flashing in his head, but then he returned Rose's gaze and said, "A brew sounds nice."

Rose led the way through the labyrinth of tents. They stepped into the mess tent, to be hit with the heat and smell of a hundred diners. Rose pointed to a space on one of the long benches. "You sit down, and I'll get us some tea."

Harry made his way over to the table, irritated there wasn't a quieter spot for them to sit. He removed his cap and tried to tidy his hair, then sank down amongst a group of rowdy orderlies. Rose appeared a moment later and placed two mugs on the table. She squeezed in next to him and took a sip of the steaming brew. "So, what's it like driving the ambulance cars?"

"Took a bit of getting used to. The roads aren't really roads. More like quagmires. And some of the sights are grim. But you'll know that of course."

She nodded and blew on the hot liquid. Harry stole a sideways look to watch her. "How long will you be on the train for?" he asked.

"Not sure. I hope I can stay. I love it." Her face glowed and for a moment he was lost in her eyes.

"There you are! I've been looking for you everywhere."

Harry twisted round to see Rose's friend from the boat. She was breathing hard, and her cheeks were pink from exertion. Rose smiled. "Amy, this is Harry. Harry, this is Amy."

Harry stood up and Amy grabbed his hand, shaking it enthusiastically. "Please to meet you, Harry. Sorry, but the train is loaded and leaving any minute. We have to go."

Rose took a quick gulp of tea then briefly touched his arm. "Sorry. See you again. Cheerio."

The women dashed away, and Harry sank back down onto the bench, trying to work out what he was feeling.

***

As fighting at Loos eased, the drivers settled back into a more bearable routine and caught up on much needed sleep. They could once again take their time over washing and shaving. Convoys still went out each day, but the torrent of dead and wounded was replaced by a steady flow. Harry realised he had been so immersed in the demands of his work, he was no longer consumed with thoughts of Mary. It was only when post and food parcels arrived from England that the familiar feelings of loss rushed back. He'd watch with a mixture of envy and sadness as the other soldiers grabbed their letters and disappeared to a quiet spot to read and absorb every word. The lucky ones with parcels would open their package as if it were Christmas, delighting in each pack of biscuits or tin of sardines. He didn't know if the men noticed he never received any post, but if they did, they didn't comment. What surprised him was that it was in fact Rose who now occupied his thoughts.

***

One day in late October, Harry was returning to headquarters, having completed his final run of the day. He was relishing the thought of a wash and some grub. He spotted an infantry unit up ahead led by an officer on horseback, so he pulled off the road into a deserted farm. As they passed, he realised the soldier riding was, in fact, a Private, clearly in a state of collapse, the officer walking alongside. Harry had witnessed similar acts of compassion by officers before. He saluted the captain and gave a nod to the soldiers. Out of the corner of his eye he caught a movement behind the farm gate and hopped down. The gate had been left open and was banging against the post. He ventured round the side of the farmhouse and saw a skinny, black dog, a mongrel by the look of it, trembling, with its tail fixed firmly between its legs.

"Hello, boy." Harry knelt down. "You all alone?"

The dog took a few steps back. His fur was dirty and matted and one of his ears had an open wound.

"It's alright, boy. Let's find you a drink." Harry tested the door handle and found it unlocked. He stepped down into the gloom of the farmhouse kitchen. Everything was in its place as though the family would be returning any minute. He tried the handle on the wrought-iron pump over the sink and, after a few splutters, a stream of brown water flowed out. He carried on pumping until the water ran clear then filled a bowl and placed it on the floor. "There you go, boy."

The dog approached cautiously and began to lap at the water. He didn't stop until the bowl was empty, then looked up and gave Harry a wag of his tail. Harry gently stroked the tangled fur then refilled the bowl. He gave him a final pat and made his way back into the yard. As he turned to close the gate, the dog had followed him out and was staring at him.

"Sorry, boy. You can't come with me." He climbed in the cab and sat for a moment. Then he leant out and looked back at the gate. The dog hadn't moved. Harry took a breath. "I think I'm going to regret this."

***

He pulled into headquarters and parked up. A group of men were kicking a ball around the yard, but the game halted the minute they saw Harry lifting a dog from his car and they gathered round to greet the new arrival.

"Who's this sorry-looking fella?" asked Frank, holding his hand out for the dog to sniff.

"I found him on a farm. Just left on his own," replied Harry, catching sight of Captain Bate striding towards them.

"Bet you're hungry, boy," said Arthur. "Let's find you something to eat."

The captain approached and singled Harry out. "A word, please, Private."

"Yes, Sir." Harry stood to attention.

"What do you think you're doing?" asked Bate.

"What do you mean, Sir?"

"Don't play dumb, Private."

"I couldn't leave him, Sir. He'd have died."

Harry realised how weak his argument sounded,

bearing in mind the loss of lives they were witnessing every day. What was one dog?

"The countryside is littered with strays, Stone. You planning on giving them all a home?"

"No, Sir."

Harry glanced across at the men fussing round the scruffy creature. Bate followed his gaze and pondered for a moment. "Alright, Stone. But get him thoroughly cleaned up. We don't want fleas adding to our problems."

"Yes, Sir. Thank you, Sir."

The captain started to walk away, then called back over his shoulder, "Looks like No.2 Convoy has a mascot."

"Yes, Sir," said Harry with a grin.

Harry scrounged some leftovers from the cook, then he and Arthur bathed and groomed the dog as best they could. They cleaned the wound on his ear. It looked like a bite.

"Been getting into fights, have you?" said Arthur. He received a sloppy lick and a wag of the tail, now clean and fluffy. Frank and Billy joined them after supper.

"What're you gonna call him?" asked Frank.

"Needs a name. Needs a name," added Billy.

"Well, he is French, so maybe a French name?" replied Harry.

"What about Napoleon? He was French," said Frank with a grin.

"And short and hairy," quipped Arthur.

The dog was now curled up at Harry's feet, eyes closed.

"Every Frenchman I meet seems to be called Jean, Jacques or Luc," said Frank, blowing out a stream of smoke.

Harry turned to him. "Luc. I like Luc."

The men nodded in agreement whilst Luc started

to snore.

**

Autumn turned into winter and the skies were permanently heavy and grey. Some roads became virtually unpassable. The drivers longed for a cold, frosty morning with a bright sky. Something to harden the slimy mud. Luc had gradually filled out and his coat was now thick and glossy. Harry had driven out to the veterinary camp and sought out one of the vets caring for the horses. He had asked him to examine Luc's ear, which didn't appear to be healing. The vet had swabbed it with an iodine tincture and given Harry a small bottle to take with him, advising careful and regular bathing of the wound. It was now fully healed with a bald patch the only evidence of injury. Luc had free rein of the farm and soon worked out if he waited by the kitchen door, it was only a matter of time before his patience would be rewarded with a tasty treat from the cook. He quickly learned to keep well clear of the cars and discovered the top of a pile of crates was the perfect vantage point for observing the comings and goings. The most exciting part of the day was when the drivers started up their engines each morning. His tailed wagged furiously and he bounced up and down next to Harry, impatient to be off.

**

It was early December when a rumour came through that a German officer had been captured and was divulging plans of an attack, but it took a couple of weeks before full details reached No.2 Convoy. The Germans were planning to launch their first phosgene attack.

"What the hell is phosgene?" asked Frank, scraping

out a tin of bully beef he had devoured.

"Another type of gas," replied Arthur, looking up from a letter he was reading. "Like chlorine gas, only worse."

"Jesus," said Frank. "It'll be U.B.C."

"At least we know now when it's coming," said Harry, sipping at a mug of hot tea.

Joseph shook his head. "Those poor devils," he said.

Billy spoke up. "I heard that the German hinted we've got a spy in our ranks." The men turned towards him in unison.

"What?"

"That's impossible."

"Ridiculous."

Arthur folded up his letter. "He's just trying to get us mistrusting each other. Anyway, listen, here's some good news for you, lads. My Flo said they had what they called a Cinema Day in November and all the takings from every cinema in Britain on that day were donated to the Red Cross Ambulance Fund."

Frank laughed and turned to Billy. "Hey Billy Billy. You might get a new car to replace that heap of rubbish you drive."

Billy looked pensive and turned to Frank. "Why do you call me Billy Billy?"

Frank gave a little chuckle and answered, "Because, mate, you say everything twice."

Billy looked confused. "No, I don't. No, I don't."

There was a moment's pause, then the group burst into laughter whilst Billy just sat scratching his head in bewilderment.

Chapter Twelve

Brushing a lock of hair from her eyes, Rose stepped down off the upturned crate to admire her handiwork. She called to Amy who was alongside the next railway carriage, thirty or so feet away. "Are you nearly finished?"

Amy wiped her hand down her front, leaving a red streak on her overall, and shouted back, "Nearly. Just a corner to do."

Rose studied the large red cross sitting in a white square on the side of the carriage. The wet paint was glistening in the winter sunshine. Tiny black dots speckled the paintwork where miniscule bugs had settled and become trapped. Rose spotted a smudge of red in the white. How annoying. She was aware of the guns booming in the distance. Amy arrived by her side and tilted her head, assessing Rose's artwork. "Not as neat as mine," she said.

Rose gave her a dig in the ribs and said, "Let's just hope it doesn't rain in the next hour or so." She knelt to replace the lid on the pot of paint, the pressure forcing more red drips to ooze down the side of the tin. They turned over the crates and placed the pots and brushes in the bottom. Amy picked hers up and made her way to the carriage door, calling over her shoulder, "I'll find Pierre and ask if he'll clean the brushes for us."

"I think Pierre would do absolutely anything you asked him to do," Rose shouted after her.

Pierre was Chief Orderly on the train and Amy had successfully charmed him and every last one of his crew. Her thick, blonde curls and pretty smile had captivated them immediately and once they heard her flawless French they were completely under her spell. It was a constant source of amusement to Rose, but she had to admit, the benefits were many. When the carriages were freezing due to a gas and electric failure, a small oil heater had magically appeared in their cabin. And when the nurses had worked twenty hours nonstop, a basin of hot water for washing was waiting for them next to their bunks. Not to mention the numerous times two mugs of cocoa had arrived as they were preparing to turn in.

The women clambered up onto the train, wrestling with their long dresses. After off-loading the last cargo of patients at Boulogne, the train had been sitting in a siding on the outskirts of Merville for the last twenty-four hours, awaiting orders. Rose hated the inactivity, especially when it was spent in some anonymous siding with the noise of rickety trains crawling past and wailing whistles sounding throughout the night. Troop trains and supply waggons took priority on the lines and the ambulance trains were fitted in where possible. Consequently, they could be on the move at a moment's notice, meaning short walks alongside the carriages were the only exercise and fresh air permitted. One of the orderlies had, not long ago, been caught out and was left buying beer from a local on the platform of a small station outside Rouen. He had re-joined the train two days later looking suitably embarrassed and shamefaced. The crew had only just stopped teasing him about it.

***

The women had been on the ambulance train for almost two months. Following the Loos offensive, they were ordered to remain with the train and "continue the good work". They couldn't have been happier. And now, instead of shunting back and forth between Saint Omer and Merville, the train was crisscrossing the French countryside, affording them shifting views and new towns to explore whenever they had the chance. Rose loved to see the scenery transform from wooded hillsides and rushing rivers to pretty villages and shining lakes. In quiet moments her thoughts would turn to Harry. She couldn't help but find his awkwardness and dishevelled appearance endearing and she wondered if he thought about her. She hoped he was safe.

***

After the nurses had washed their hands and faces and removed the dirty overalls, they made their way to the small dining car for lunch. The rest of the staff were already seated and had been joined by two French officials whom Rose hadn't seen before. The mood seemed light, and conversation was flowing. Rose placed herself alongside Sister Burton. She had developed a great respect for the Senior Sister and admired her methods and leadership. Two orderlies arrived carrying bowls of potage and crusty bread. Within minutes, Amy was dazzling the French visitors with her language skills and Rose felt a rush of affection for her. She turned to Major Colton. "When do you think we'll be moving up, Major?"

Colton placed his spoon down. "Soon I would think. The clearing stations at Merville are overflowing by all accounts."

Rose nodded and took another mouthful of stew. She was struggling to identify the meat content, perhaps for the best, but it was nevertheless a tasty dish. Suddenly there was a succession of loud bangs of artillery fire, causing the windows to rattle, followed by what sounded like a roll of thunder.

"The wind must be in our direction," said Fitzpatrick, glancing out the window. He was a wiry man with thinning hair and had the endearing habit, Rose had noticed, of addressing the nurses as 'fine ladies'.

Sister Green began to recount a story a young officer had told her, and the diners turned to listen. "He and six of his men were scouting an abandoned village and they came across a barn which he thought could be used as a billet. But when they went inside it was full of dead women and children. And…" The nurse hesitated and looked down at her lap. She took a deep breath and continued, "And none of them had any hands."

Everyone was quiet.

"Damned Hun," said Colton, his face clouding with anger.

Amy spoke up. "I've been hearing that German snipers are shooting stretcher bearers."

The French officials shook their heads and mumbled some obscenities. They quickly apologised when they saw Amy blushing.

"I've been told by more than one patient that the Germans will raise a white flag as if to surrender and when our boys approach, they shoot them," said one of the other nurses.

"And they transport guns and artillery on trains with red crosses on them 'cos they know we won't bomb them, even though they bomb ours," added Amy.

Rose looked out of the window. It made for grim listening. Two orderlies reappeared carrying small glasses of delicious-smelling coffee and wedges of cheese. Rose noticed the largest piece of cheese landed in front of Amy. The mood at the table gradually lifted and conversation moved on. But Rose couldn't shake off the image of piles of handless women and children. What would possess someone to commit that kind of act, even during a war? She would never comprehend it.

***

Orders came through later that afternoon. They were to load up at Merville and drop off at Rouen. Rose hoped there would be time to catch the tram into the city. She was desperate for a bath and shampoo and Rouen had the cleanest public baths she'd come across. They had just finished supper when she felt the train creak and grind into action. It juddered and clanked its way out of the siding onto the main line. The light had faded and all she could see was an expanse of empty blackness. It wasn't until the train rounded a bend that the sky was no longer black but alight with flashes and explosions. Time and again the horizon lit up with bright, white bursts of light. Some streaked across the sky, others erupted into a star of intense brilliance. Rose had seen such displays many times, but it never ceased to enthral her. Or make her wonder what horrors now lay beneath the dazzling show?

***

Merville station was the usual sea of khaki. Fresh troops arriving from the ports were congregating on the concourse. Medical officers were shouting instructions and walking wounded were milling around. Loading completed, the train clanked out of the station and crawled its way to Rouen.

The patients were unloaded amid calls of "Thank you, Nurse" and "See you in Blighty". As the final soldier was carried off down the platform, the nurses collapsed on the nearest bunk, happy and relieved that not one patient had been lost. Sister Burton appeared in the carriage.

"Well done, ladies. Let's get the bunks stripped and remade. The blankets are being offloaded here for fumigation and all being well, we should receive a new supply later. Orders are to move out this evening, so you have a few hours if you'd like to go into the city."

There was a chorus of cheers.

***

The six nurses, each clutching a washbag, negotiated the busy streets, sidestepping the pedestrians filling the pavements. Rose would have loved to explore the ancient thoroughfares and half-timbered buildings, but her priority was a bath. This could be the last chance she'd get for who knew how long.

The women spent a blissful hour bathing and shampooing, then bought coffee and cake in a crowded café looking out onto the twin spires and intricate architecture of Rouen cathedral. As Rose sipped the bitter coffee, she looked round the table at the women she now called friends and smiled to herself. She suddenly spotted the grumpy waiter winding his way through the packed tables towards them. "Think we've outstayed our welcome, girls. Let's go."

They gathered their things and made a quick exit, managing to jump straight onto a tram heading back to the station.

Chapter Thirteen

"Good morning, Celeste. You're very chatty this morning."

The canary hopped from one perch to the other and continued to chirp, giving a quick shake of her daffodil feathers. Amy appeared at Rose's side. "*En Francais!* She's French, Rose. You have to speak to her in French." Amy put her face up to the cage. *"Bonjour, Celeste. Tu chantes comme une ange ce matin."*

"Perhaps I'm teaching her English."

Amy snorted. "You're just confusing her."

"She doesn't understand, you know."

Amy looked shocked. "Of course she does!" She leant forward again. *"N'est-ce pas, ma petite?"*

Rose shook her head. "I'll take her down to No. 4 carriage." She lifted the cage and made her way along the train, the little bird singing all the way.

She had heard stories of canaries on board ambulance trains and nurses reporting dramatic changes in the mood of the soldiers who loved the birdsong and the company. She had forgotten she'd mentioned it to the orderlies until the beautiful bird miraculously appeared in her cabin ten days later. The resourcefulness of her French colleagues never ceased to amaze her. Amy had immediately named the bird Celeste because, she explained, it meant 'heavenly', and the canary sang like an angel.

The train had been stuck in a siding outside Etaples for twenty-four hours, waiting to unload. The lines were full of troop trains moving up to Merville and Bailleul. With Christmas approaching, Rose was hoping these casualties at least would be back in England in time for the twenty-fifth. Every bunk was filled and as Rose moved through the carriages, she was greeted with smiles and requests for the cage to be left there.

"No. 4 carriage today, gentlemen," she said. She left a tide of grumbles in her wake. No.4 had the most serious cases. One soldier had lost both legs, another his left arm and foot. Everyone's eyes lit up when she entered, cage in hand.

"Your turn to have Celeste keep you company, gentlemen," she said, smiling broadly.

"That's grand, Nurse," said a private, propping himself up to be able to whistle through the cage. The bird immediately chirped and twittered in reply. Rose placed the cage down and returned along the train to begin the morning tasks of changing dressings, checking wounds, and administering medicines.

Amy was on duty in the Infectious Ward at the end of the train. She was nursing a corporal called Miller, racked with fever and hallucinating. One minute he thought she was his mother, the next he was back at the Front. He grabbed her hand, clutching it with an iron grip, his eyes wild and staring.

"I've got fifty dead men to bury," he said.

Amy mopped his forehead and tried to calm him but then he suddenly sat up and pointed down the carriage.

"There's a German spy. Stop him, stop him."

Amy gently lay him back down. "It's alright, Corporal. They've caught him. Lie down and rest."

The ramblings continued hour after hour.

***

Rose hadn't realised it was lunchtime until the orderlies arrived carrying mugs of thick broth. She and the other nurses helped those soldiers who couldn't feed themselves, before gathering for their own meal. They were laughing about their bad-tempered engine driver when Amy appeared, wiping her eyes. "We lost Corporal

Miller."

Rose took her hand and gently pulled her down into the seat next to her. Amy sniffed and rubbed a tear off her cheek. "I don't know why I'm so upset."

"It's alright, Amy," said one of the other nurses. "We can't be immune to it all the time. It's not possible."

Amy nodded and picked up one of the napkins to dry her eyes.

"She's right, Amy," said Rose. "Don't be so hard on yourself."

Amy blew her nose. "He was engaged to be married."

They encouraged her to eat some of her soup and were just finishing coffee when Sister Burton appeared. She gave Amy a reassuring pat on the shoulder.

"You've worked hard this morning, ladies. And it's not been an easy morning." She paused. "But on a lighter note, Major Colton has suggested we brighten up the train with some Christmas decorations."

The nurses looked at each other excitedly. Even Amy managed a weak smile. The Sister continued. "As soon as we've unloaded at Etaples, I'll ask Pierre if he can dash into the town and find us some festive bits and pieces."

***

It was mid-afternoon when the train clunked and rattled its way out of the siding and finally crawled into Etaples station. The platforms were, as ever, seething with soldiers and casualties. Stretcher bearers emerged from the throng and the slow process of unloading began once more. Rose spotted Pierre disappearing into the crowd. Another mission. Christmas was only three days away but there was little evidence of the festive season in the station. She wondered how her parents would find Christmas without her. She pictured the tree in its customary position in the bay window and stockings hanging from the mantlepiece. She felt a sudden, unexpected rush of homesickness and for a moment wished she was back in the front room, with her mother sitting on the sofa doing her embroidery and her father hidden behind his newspaper, a puff of smoke from his pipe occasionally drifting up from behind the pages.

She heard a voice behind her.

"Can you take these sheets off me, Rose, and I'll go and fetch some more." It was Amy carrying a pile of clean bedding for the bunks. She shoved them into Rose's arms and retreated up the carriage towards the storeroom.

By the time the train was empty of patients and the beds remade, Pierre had returned, laden with greenery, holly, and coloured paper. He'd worked his magic yet again. The nurses eagerly began to adorn the carriages. Rose and Amy took on the task of creating yards and yards of paper chains. Even the medical officers were draping garlands. Someone started to hum 'The Holly and the Ivy' and before long the train was filled with the sound of carols. Rose became aware of a deep harmony amongst the voices and realised it was Major Fitzpatrick. She smiled across at him and he stopped, blushing slightly.

"Church choir. First tenor," he said.

"You have a beautiful voice, Sir."

***

It was late evening when orders came through to proceed to Rouen. There had been a call to clear the hospitals in the city to make space for wounded coming directly from the Front. The train would then head to Boulogne to a waiting hospital ship.

"Ooh, I hope we can get on board for a bath," said

Amy, struggling to get a brush through her tangle of curls. "My hair is such a mess."

"Mine too," said Rose, climbing into her narrow bunk. "Maybe it'll be a Christmas Day bath."

Amy laughed. "A seasonal soak!"

"That sounds nice," said Rose sleepily. She pulled up the covers and closed her eyes, drifting off to the sway of the train as it trundled slowly towards Rouen.

***

It was, in fact, Christmas Eve before the nurses were able to enjoy the luxury of a bath. The journey had taken most of the night and it was another twenty-four hours before the last patient was unloaded in Boulogne. The seven nurses and two medical officers navigated the busy quay. They had been given permission to make use of the bathrooms on board the hospital ship Asturias. The docks ran parallel to each other, and Rose gazed across at the warships and troop carriers sitting side by side in the narrow channels. Every quayside was teeming with soldiers, horses, and supply trucks. The group reached the gangplank and waited for permission to board. The Asturias had been a Royal Mail steamship but had been requisitioned by the Royal Navy. Rose looked up at the tall masts either end of the ship and the large oval funnel in the middle. It could not have been a more welcome sight.

***

The train was to return to Rouen which meant no time for shopping or sightseeing. And no time to visit the Paymaster's office. Rose hoped the few francs she had left would last until the next visit to the city. Everyone was back on board within a couple of hours, soaked, scrubbed, and shampooed.

As the train clanked its way out of the port, they gathered for supper, the fresh smell of soap in the air. Rose was sitting next to Major Colton. She detected a hint of cologne and noticed his moustache had been trimmed and combed. She respected the medical officers enormously and enjoyed working alongside them both.

"Where did you train, Major?" she asked, taking a bite of the crusty bread.

"St George's," replied Colton, wiping his mouth on his napkin.

"Ah, a 'Corner Man'," said Rose.

The Major smiled. "You've heard of us then?"

"Yes, but never met one of you." Rose had heard the term whilst she was training, referring to the fact St George's Hospital was situated on Hyde Park Corner.

"Never thought I'd be practising medicine on a train in Northern France," said Colton.

At that moment, Pierre and two other orderlies appeared carrying plates of hot roast pork and potatoes. All three of them had wide grins on their faces.

"Une surprise pour vous," announced Pierre. "Surprise. For the Christmas."

Everyone's eyes lit up and there was a chorus of thank yous from around the tables.

"Merci beaucoup, Pierre. Vous êtes très gentil," said Amy with a twinkle in her eye. Pierre turned a shade of pink and retreated out of the carriage. The air was soon filled with the aroma of herbs and roast meat. The pork was followed by plum pudding and coffee. Fitzpatrick disappeared briefly, returning a few minutes later holding a bottle of rum. Amy quickly drained her coffee and held out the glass.

"Amy!" exclaimed Rose. She turned to see Sister

Burton's reaction.

"It's Christmas." said Amy, still holding her glass aloft. All eyes were on Sister.

"Alright, ladies. Sister Turner's right. It is Christmas and there will be little time for celebrations tomorrow." Everyone drained their glasses of coffee.

"Splendid," said Fitzpatrick. He opened the bottle and went round the table pouring a tot in each glass.

"If I could make a toast, please?" The Major cleared his throat. "I'm sure we all wish we could be with our family at this time. But we are doing vital work and our brave boys need us. It is a pleasure working with you fine ladies and you, Major Colton. Merry Christmas and God Save the King."

Everyone rose and raised their glasses.

"God Save the King."

***

By the time Rose climbed into bed, her head was spinning, and she was desperate to sleep. As she turned out the lamp, she felt the train come to a juddering halt. Another delay. It quickly became obvious they were alongside a cattle truck packed with dozens of raucous pigs. Rose pulled the covers over her head, but the snorting and grunting continued through the night. She couldn't help thinking it was some sort of retribution for the roast pork she had enjoyed at supper.

***

Christmas Day brought the usual heavy workload and multitude of wounds and illnesses. It also brought orders for Rose. She was to leave the ambulance train and had been assigned to No. 2 Casualty Clearing Station in

Bailleul. Amy was distraught.

"How can they separate us?" she wailed. "It's not fair."

"I'm sure we'll be working together again soon," said Rose, her arm around Amy's shoulders.

"You don't know that," said Amy, wiping tears from her cheeks. "What am I going to do without you?"

"You'll be so busy, you'll soon get used to not having me here."

Amy shook her head. "Never."

Rose laughed and gave her friend a hug. "I'm going to miss you."

Chapter Fourteen

Harry had unloaded at the clearing station and was free to grab something to eat and drink. The air was bitter, and he could barely feel his fingers even with the heavy leather gloves. He had parked his car and was putting on his coat, Luc at his feet, when he heard a voice.

"So, you have a co-driver now?"

He spun round and saw Rose, laden down with blankets and smiling broadly at him. He stepped towards her, his heart pounding.

"Rose!"

"Hello again. Who is this?"

"This is Luc." Luc trotted forward, tail wagging.

"Hello, Luc. You are very handsome. Sorry I can't give you a pat." She grabbed awkwardly at one of the blankets as it threatened to slip off the top of the pile.

"Can I help you with those?" asked Harry, stepping forward.

"Thank you," said Rose. "I'm heading this way."

Harry ordered a disappointed Luc back into the cab, promising to bring him a treat.

"Can't he come?" asked Rose.

"Better not. He'll be fine."

She set off briskly through the maze of tents with Harry following close behind, his mind whirring. When she paused outside the Moribund tent, he hesitated.

"You're working here?"

She nodded and studied him for a moment.

"I'll take them off you here, if you like?"

"No, it's fine. Lead the way."

They ducked into the tent and crossed to the nurses' station. Harry detected the unmistakable smell of gangrene and fought the urge to wretch. Rose dumped the blankets on a large table alongside some pillows and other supplies and relieved him of his load. A senior sister was sitting writing at a desk. She looked up and eyed Harry, then Rose.

"Right, Sister Davidson, think it might be time for a tea break," she said. "Would you mind bringing one back for me?"

Rose looked at her in surprise. "Of course, Sister."

"One sugar, please." The Sister resumed her work. "No rush."

This time they were able to find a quiet table in the far corner of the tent. Rose fetched the tea once again, along with a plate of biscuits.

"Thought you could take some of these for Luc," she said.

"He'll be your friend for ever," said Harry.

She stepped over the bench and dropped down next to him. He picked up one of the biscuits and studied the familiar grid of holes and lettering.

"I used to work for Huntley and Palmers," he said.

"Really?" said Rose in surprise.

"In Reading. My father worked there all his life and I joined when I left school. That's where I learnt to drive."

She rested her hand on her chin. Harry tapped the biscuit on the table. "Have to watch your teeth on these things, you know?"

She smiled. "Are your parents still in Reading?"

Harry shook his head. "No. They've passed away. Tuberculosis."

"Oh, I'm sorry."

He gave a little shrug. "It was a long time ago. So, where are you from?"

"London. Holborn. My father works in a bank and my mother has taken on the job of finding me an eligible bachelor to marry."

Harry raised his eyebrows, a flicker of concern

running through him. Rose continued.

"She successfully married off my sister and turned her attentions to me. At one point there was a steady stream of them, invited for afternoon tea. Sons and nephews of friends and acquaintances." She paused. "A couple of them were nice enough, but all I wanted to do was become a nurse, much to my mother's horror."

"So how did you manage to convince her?"

"I convinced my father first."

"Ah. And he did the rest."

"She couldn't keep up with the disapproval for ever and in fact, by the time I completed my training I think she was actually quite proud of me. I even overheard her defending me to one of her snobby friends, describing the 'invaluable work carried out by nurses during the Boer War'."

"She should be proud of you," said Harry. Rose blushed.

"Well, I'm sure Sister will be wondering where her tea is." She stood up from the bench. "Don't forget the biscuits for Luc." She handed him the treats. "Cheerio."

A few minutes later Harry climbed into his cab. Luc greeted him excitedly sniffing at his pocket. "There you go, boy. A present from Rose." He held out the biscuits and Luc devoured them in seconds then settled back into the footwell. Harry sat for a moment, images of Mary running through his head, wondering what she would think.

***

It was mild day with the sun attempting to break through the cloud cover. Harry heard the splutter of the aeroplane before he could see it. He craned his neck and searched the sky. It suddenly came into view, the drone of the engine growing steadily louder. He couldn't tell if it was friend or foe. The plane circled around, and Harry recognised the familiar shape of a German Taube. It banked low and headed back towards the front line, reconnaissance completed. As he watched it retreating to the north, the sky around it was peppered with bursts of gunfire. He held his breath. Somehow the plane weathered the barrage and disappeared into the distance. He bent down and gave Luc a pat. "They'll get him next time, eh boy?"

Arthur appeared at his side. "Are we off then? Let's make the most of this free time and see if we can find a beer."

Half an hour later, the men were sitting in a small *estaminet* on the outskirts of the town, two glasses of pale beer on the table in front of them. The owner was a scruffy, bearded man with a loud voice and an even louder laugh. He greeted his customers with a torrent of high velocity French ending with belly-deep laughter. From the small amount of French Harry had picked up, he seemed to be castigating and belittling the Germans and, not surprisingly, wishing all kinds of ill to befall them.

"He's enjoying his own jokes," said Harry, taking a gulp of beer. He retrieved a pack of cigarettes from his pocket and passed one to Arthur. There was a steady flow of customers, all in uniform of one kind or another. He detected the soft drawl of a Canadian accent coming from the table behind them. A couple of nurses walking past the café window caught his eye and he twisted in his seat to get a better look.

"It's not her," said Arthur, blowing out a stream of smoke.

"Who?" said Harry, turning back round.

"The girl from the boat."

"You mean Rose."

"Yes. Rose." Arthur paused. "Are you going to see her again?"

Harry's head came up. "What? No. Course not."

"Why not?"

"No point. We'd never get to see each other." He brushed some crumbs from his lap, whilst Arthur eyed him suspiciously. "You're telling me you're not interested?"

"Just don't think it would be worth the effort," replied Harry, avoiding Arthur's gaze.

Arthur stubbed out his cigarette. "Well, if you want my advice, I think she's totally worth the effort. Listen, Harry …."

He was interrupted by the arrival of a group of Australian soldiers, all wearing the distinctive slouch hat with one side of the brim pinned up. The café owner welcomed them and rushed around shifting chairs and tables to try and accommodate them all. A couple of them glanced across at Harry and Arthur and gave them a nod and a 'g'day'. The noise level had increased ten-fold.

"Can't hear myself think. Let's go," said Harry, glad of an excuse to halt the conversation. Draining their glasses, they picked up their caps and cigarettes and zigzagged between the tables to the exit. As they closed the door behind them, the owner had begun to sing, bringing a raucous cheer from the delighted Australians.

They left the noise and chaos of the bar behind and with time on their hands, strolled into the town centre. Passing the Church of Saint Peter, Harry gazed up at the twin, red-brick towers looming above them, guarding the church entrance like sentries.

"Let's find something to eat," said Arthur. "That beer's made me peckish."

They continued along the street until the smell of

101

freshly baked bread led them to a small bakery at the end of the row of buildings where the road opened out into a square. As they approached, Harry couldn't believe his eyes when he saw Rose walking towards them. She was carrying a basket loaded with provisions and reading what looked to be a shopping list. They were almost in front of her before she looked up.

"Harry!"

The soldiers removed their caps. "Hello, Rose," said Harry. He felt a nudge from Arthur. "Rose, may I introduce Arthur. Arthur, this is Rose."

"I finally get to meet you," said Arthur, shaking her hand.

"Pleasure to meet you, Arthur. Are you a driver too?"

"Yes, I am. I have the dubious honour of working with this fine fellow here." His eyes were twinkling, and Harry flashed him a warning glance.

"Well, I'm going to buy some of that delicious-smelling bread the French are so good at. Lovely to meet you, Rose." He donned his cap, gave Harry a surreptitious wink and stepped into the shop.

Harry gave a little laugh. "I think he may have got the wrong idea about us."

Rose looked up at him, her face serious. "Has he?"

His smile disappeared and he looked away, unable to answer.

"Is there someone else, Harry? Someone waiting for you at home…?"

"No, there's no one else. It's just…" Was he ready to talk about Mary? His heart was racing.

"Just what?" asked Rose.

"It's difficult to explain." He willed himself to say the words he knew she wanted to hear, but the image of Mary held him back. Rose glanced down, sighed, then looked straight into his eyes.

"I thought perhaps there was something between us, but clearly I was mistaken," she continued, "I obviously misread the situation and I apologise if I've embarrassed you. Good day." With that, she turned on her heels and vanished round the corner.

Harry cursed and slapped his cap against his thigh. Fool. Arthur emerged from the bakery with two baguettes tucked under his arm. When he saw Harry's face, his shoulders sank.

"What have you done?"

***

Harry spent the night replaying the conversation and wishing he'd handled it differently. He went round and round in circles, always to return to the same image each time. Mary standing in the kitchen. He should never have gone to work that day. It was the early hours of the morning before tiredness took over and he fell into a dreamless sleep.

***

The following day, he drove towards the clearing station full of apprehension. What if he bumped into her? He pulled off the road and into the field. Some black specks appeared on the horizon. They looked like a distant flock of birds, and he peered through the grimy windscreen to look more closely. The specks grew larger. Planes returning from a reconnaissance flight. Ahead of him, an ambulance had become bogged down and was blocking the track, a queue of cars behind it. Four drivers were attempting a rescue mission and he jumped out to see if he could help, Luc close behind him. He joined the men at the back of the vehicle grunting and groaning as they put all their weight into trying to shift it, but the wheels continued to spin in the mire.

"We need something around the tyres, branches maybe," said one of them. They headed towards the nearby hedgerow and began to break off as much brush as they could, dragging it back to the stranded car. The drone of the aeroplanes was louder now.

"Try again," yelled a voice. The engine revved and the wheels sent branches and twigs catapulting out from behind the tyres.

"We need more," said Harry, turning to watch the planes pass over, but as he raised his hand above his eyes to block out the brightness, a black cross came slowly into focus and his blood turned to ice. He watched as a dark object fell ominously from the lead plane and seconds later a mass of earth and smoke erupted from below in a deafening explosion. Luc started to bark. The group of drivers turned and looked in horror at the scene below them.

Another bomb dropped and they could hear screaming and shouting echoing up the hill. The men were frozen to the spot. Luc barked again and Harry came to his senses. My God, Rose. Panic surged through him, and he began to run, Luc at his heels, willing his legs to go faster. More explosions ripped through the camp, and he felt the ground shaking. As each bomb fell, his fear of losing Rose mounted. What had he been thinking? Why hadn't he just been honest? With Rose and with himself. He raced down the hill, almost losing his footing, until he reached the edge of the camp.

The once neat rows were now a mass of tattered canvas and bodies. Fire and smoke filled the air and cries of agony surrounded him. He sprinted through the chaos, jumping, and swerving to avoid the wreckage, Luc still at his side. Finally, he reached what was left of the

Moribund tent and stopped in his tracks. Mangled corpses littered the ground and he gagged on the smell of burnt flesh. He glimpsed a nurse's uniform buried under some rubble and started grabbing at the debris, throwing it to one side. A lifeless face appeared. He darted to the next body, twisted and blackened. It wasn't Rose. He looked around in despair. Where was she? Panic-stricken and terrified, he stood up and screamed her name.

Chapter Fifteen

The planes had passed over, their deathly drone fading away. Harry continued to scrabble through the carnage, but found only patients, none of them alive. Perhaps Rose hadn't been there. Sent off on another errand.

A medical officer rushed up to him. "Any survivors?"

"No, Sir."

"Right, I'll find you some help and you can get these bodies lined up ready for identification and collection."

Harry turned full circle, scanning the devastated camp.

"Did you hear me, Private?" asked the officer.

Where could she be?

"Private."

Harry jumped.

"Wake up, man. Get to it."

"Yes, Sir."

But he stood rooted to the spot, his mind racing and a sickening fear gripping his stomach. An orderly approached and nodded a greeting. He surveyed the scene and shook his head. "Damn those Huns." Harry turned and stared blankly at him, aware of a voice but not listening to the words.

"You alright, mate?" asked the orderly.

Harry forced himself to concentrate. "Yes...yes, fine."

The two men worked together to clear the area and retrieve the casualties. Luc had distanced himself and lay watching the grim process. By the time they had finished, the row of dead stretched for twenty yards, a grisly line of burnt and broken bodies. A nurse had appeared with a supply of blankets and had taken on the task of removing identification discs, checking for personal items, and covering the corpses. When Harry quizzed her, she said she knew Rose, but had not seen her since the raid.

After the deafening explosions and the screaming and

shouting, the camp had now taken on an eerie calm. The shock and horror had receded and the task of caring for the wounded had resumed. Ambulance cars were arriving to transport the dead and injured and the nurse hurried away to record the names and details of the deceased. Sensing Harry's agitation, the orderly offered to wait until all the bodies had been collected. Harry voiced his thanks and set off through the camp, Luc at his heels once again.

Emergency treatment areas had been hastily set up and he sprinted from one to another, hurriedly searching the stricken faces. He overheard a nurse saying soup was being handed out. Miraculously, the mess had escaped with minimal damage and a queue of weary people was trailing out of the entrance. Harry went along the line asking if anyone had seen Rose, but he was met with shaking heads. Where was she?

As he stood forlornly, an officer appeared. "What are you doing, Private?"

Harry couldn't think what to say.

"Are you a driver?" asked the officer.

"Yes, Sir, ambulance."

"Where's your vehicle?"

"At the top of the hill, Sir."

"Well, don't just stand there. Get to your car and start helping. We're evacuating to No 8." The man gave him a hard look, then hurried away.

Harry trudged up the field, a stream of cars passing him. The stranded ambulance had been freed and the way was clear for the convoy of vehicles. Luc hopped into the cab and Harry followed. He drove steadily back down the slope, fear for Rose engulfing him. All the doubt and hesitation. Punishing himself for so long. Did he deserve a second chance? All he knew was the thought of Rose being injured, or worse, was unbearable.

He took on some of the last casualties and transported them across the town. As he helped to unload, he spotted Dev rushing towards him.

"We've been looking for you," he said, "Arthur's seen Rose."

Harry grabbed his arm. "Where is she? Is she alright?"

"Yes, she's alright. Cuts and burns, but alright." He gave Harry a smile. "She's on the far side of the camp."

Harry thanked him and raced off. He dashed from tent to tent until finally, he saw her. She was sitting on a bench alongside other walking wounded, her face ashen and streaked with tears and dirt. One hand was holding a dressing against her cheek, whilst the other rested on her lap covered with a cloth. Her uniform was torn and soiled, with dried blood forming streaks down the front. He rushed forward and knelt in front of her. As she looked at him, her eyes filled with more tears.

"They're gone. They're all gone."

"I know."

Her head fell forward onto his shoulder, and he held her while she wept. Eventually, he sat her up and wiped her eyes.

"Let me take a look at your face," he said. She removed the dressing to reveal a deep gash running across her cheek.

"I'm waiting for it to be stitched," she said, sounding more composed.

"And what about your hand?"

She lifted the cloth, wincing. The skin was a vivid red with patches of peeling skin and her shirt cuff had been burnt away. Harry carefully covered it. "You're going to be fine. You'll be nursing again before you know it."

She nodded and wiped her face on her sleeve. A medical officer appeared at Harry's side.

"Time for you to go, Private."

Raising himself up he took her face in his hands and said, "I'll come back as soon as I can." He bent forward and kissed the top of her head. "I promise."

A few yards away Carter was on his way back to his ambulance, and he had witnessed the whole exchange.

Chapter Sixteen

Three long weeks passed before Harry had leave and could seek Rose out. It was a bright spring day with a hint of summer. The ground had dried, and the road surface was now a cracked glaze of hardened mud. He hitched a lift with Frank who was collecting patients from No. 8 and delivering them to a hospital barge in Merville.

"Meet you back here in a couple of hours?" he said.

Frank wished him luck and slammed the car into gear.

***

After questioning several nurses, Harry managed to find one who knew of Rose and was directed to a tent housing patients recovering from surgery. He stepped inside and scanned the rows of bunks, every one of them occupied. In the far corner, Rose was sitting next to a bed, reading aloud. Harry's heart skipped a beat, and he watched her unnoticed for a moment. The dressing had been removed from her cheek but even from a distance he could see the red welt running down from her left eye. Her hand was still bandaged. She was in a plain dress, rather than uniform, with a ponytail hanging at the nape of her neck. Her features were animated as she brought the story to life and Harry could see the soldier was mesmerised. He approached slowly and was almost by her side before she looked up.

"Harry!" Her face lit up. She turned to the patient and lightly touched his shoulder. "Please excuse me, won't you?"

"That's alright, nurse." The soldier grinned. "No rush, I'm not going anywhere."

Harry resisted the urge to grab her hand and pull her away. Away from the blood and suffering. Away from

110

the missing limbs and sightless eyes. Away from the pervading smell of death and decay.

She headed out and Harry followed her to a quiet spot on the edge of the station where the land dropped away to pastures and trees. Neither of them spoke, and as the sounds of the camp died away, Rose turned and flung her arms around him. They stood wrapped in each other. A silent exchange of hearts.

Eventually she relaxed her hold and looked up at Harry, her eyes as bright as he'd ever seen them. He brushed a lock of hair from her face and returned her gaze. Then he leant forward and gently kissed her. He felt her respond, pressing against him, and the kiss became long and fervent. When they finally drew apart, Harry knew his heart had been captured.

"Is your face sore?" he asked.

She touched her cheek self-consciously. "It's healing well but my hand is still painful."

Harry kissed her again and she laughed. "That definitely helps."

"So when will you start nursing duties?"

"Next week with any luck. I can't wait, but the MO wants to be sure there's no infection."

"You're keeping busy by the looks of it."

"I'm doing what I can. Mostly just reading or keeping the patients company."

Harry pulled her towards him. "That chap couldn't take his eyes off you. Not that I blame him, of course."

"Are you jealous, Private Stone?"

"Maybe."

She laughed, then looked thoughtful. "Do you fancy helping me to pick lavender?"

Harry looked at her questioningly.

"We sew little sachets, fill them with lavender then pin them to the patient's pillow. It helps to mask the ghastly smells for them."

"And where do we find this lavender?"

"There's a *manoir* on the edge of the town with the most beautiful garden full of lavender and the owner says we can pick as much as we need."

"Then lead the way, *Mademoiselle*."

***

The house was situated on a quiet street in what looked to Harry to be a wealthy part of town. Its sandy-coloured stonework contrasted with the cream windowpanes. An elegant flight of steps led up to the front door. Three attic windows peeked out from the slate roof and a couple of slim chimneys towered behind them.

Rose pushed open the gate and stepped into the garden. Harry followed, ducking under the branch of a cherry tree. Its last few blossom petals sat stubbornly amongst the bright green of the spring foliage. He straightened and gazed at the scene in front of him. A pristine lawn edged with lavender bushes surrounded the house and trees and shrubs formed a barrier from the outside world. Rose swung round and beckoned him to follow. The lavender was alive with bees, and butterflies danced amongst the waving stems. Harry could smell the distinctive aroma where her dress had brushed the purple flowers. He gazed at her standing among the blooms.

"Isn't it beautiful?" she said.

"Intoxicating," he replied.

Rose moved towards him and stood on tiptoes as if to kiss him. He closed his eyes and leant down, only to feel his cap whipped from his head. She laughed and darted away, calling over her shoulder, "We need something to put the lavender in."

Grinning, he hurried to catch up with her. He spotted

movement in one of the ground floor windows and nudged Rose, nodding towards the house. An elderly woman was waving at them.

"Oh, that's Madame Dubois." She waved back enthusiastically and shouted, *"Bonjour, Madame Dubois."*

They wandered through the garden picking just a few stems from each plant. A light breeze rippled through the trees. Only when it changed direction could Harry detect the familiar thump of shell fire in the distance.

He heard footsteps on the gravel in front of the house and a moment later Madame Dubois appeared, laden down with a large tray holding cups and saucers and a plate of delicate cakes, baked golden.

"Bonjour, mes amis. Voilà, un café pour vous."

The tray was gradually tipping, sending the saucers sliding to one side and Harry rushed forward to rescue them. "May I help you with that, *Madame*?"

Rose greeted the woman with two alternate pecks on each cheek. *"Merci, Madame. Vous êtes très gentille.* Very kind."

The woman smiled at them both. *"De rien. De rien."*

"Et merci pour la lavende," continued Rose.

"N'importe quoi pour les soldats. Ils sont si courageux."

"Yes, they're incredibly brave."

The woman pointed at Rose's bandaged hand. *"Comment va votre main?"*

"A little sore." Rose pulled a face to indicate the pain.

"Ah, ma pauvre."

She glanced at Harry then back at Rose, a twinkle in her eye. *"Il est beau, n'est pas?"*

Rose looked at Harry. "Yes. Yes, he is."

He blushed but recovered quickly. "And I am also very lucky to be here with two beautiful women. *Deux belles femmes."*

The woman chuckled and waved at the tray. "*Alors, café!*" She turned and made her way back round to the front of the house.

They sat on the lawn sipping the coffee, the cap now overflowing with lavender. Harry could have stayed there for ever. He had no idea when he would be able to see her again. She could be sent back to Saint Omer or reassigned to the ambulance train. He sighed and Rose turned to him, sensing his thoughts. A tear glistened in the corner of her eye and Harry took her face in his hands. "As soon as I have leave, I'll come and see you again."

She nodded and leant into his shoulder. They sat in silence with just the sound of the bees around them.

***

Harry managed to catch a ride with Frank on his final run. The patients had all been safely transferred and the vehicle was now a taxi for two nurses and a medical officer who were on leave and heading for the train station at Merville. Harry squeezed in the back with the nurses and tried to get comfortable between the stretcher racks, whilst the officer sat up front with Frank. The women were giddy at the prospect of seeing family again and talked non-stop for the length of the journey. Harry listened, fully expecting to feel a pang of homesickness at any moment. But it never came. His life was here now and after the war, it would be with Rose and wherever she wanted to be.

The car pulled up outside the station and the passengers jumped out. The nurses dashed away, waving, and calling a thank you, whilst the officer took a moment to shake Frank's hand.

"Cheerio. Keep up the good work."

"Yes, Sir."

He picked up his case and disappeared into the crowds. Harry took his place in the cab where Frank sat for a moment looking at him.

"What are you waiting for?" asked Harry.

"Had a pleasant day?"

"Very pleasant, thank you. Shall we go?"

"I must say, you're smelling rather sweet."

"What do you mean?"

"Well, it's not the usual stink of sweat and blood."

Harry glanced down at the cap on his lap then held it up for Frank to sniff. "You mean this?"

"Why does your cap smell of lavender?"

"Just drive."

Frank grinned and pressed the accelerator.

***

Half an hour later, they pulled into the yard at headquarters. Luc bounded across to greet them.

"I am bloody starving," said Frank. "You eating?"

"No, thanks."

"Great, I'll have your rations too, then. Let's hope it's stew."

He strode off, his bulky frame filling the doorway as he stepped inside. Harry spotted Arthur sitting reading in the late sunshine. He walked up and dropped on to the ground next to him. Luc lay down and rested his head on his leg. Arthur closed his book. "Well?"

Harry paused for a moment. "You were right."

"Well, I'm not going to say, 'I told you so'," said Arthur. He passed over a cigarette. "Is she staying at No. 8?"

"For now, but who knows? She could get new orders

115

at any time."

"When will you see her again?"

"Your guess is as good as mine."

"It'll be worth it though, eh?"

"Damn right," said Harry, giving Luc a pat on the head.

Chapter Seventeen

It was a warm evening in mid-June and the men were outside enjoying the lingering daylight. Some were sitting on chairs brought from indoors, others perched on crates or sprawled on the dusty ground. All were exhausted but reluctant to turn in. Harry leant back in his chair and looked around him. Arthur was engrossed in writing a letter, a cigarette dangling from his lips. Frank, Joseph, and Billy were playing a loud and argumentative game of cards whilst Dev was throwing sticks for Luc, who never tired of a session of 'fetch'. Although Harry longed to see Rose, as he watched the men he lived and worked with, he felt a sense of contentment, a feeling he'd not experienced for a long time and a surprising one, considering his days were filled with the sights and sounds of war.

His gaze drifted in the direction of the Front. For once the guns were quiet. Harry had a vision of a caged monster that had roared for days and weeks and was now silent. Spent. Gathering its strength to begin all over again, never to be freed from its suffering.

Joseph's voice interrupted his reverie. "Fancy a go on the motorcycle?"

He straightened up. "Really?"

Joseph nodded. "I'll talk you through it and you can have a bash."

Harry jumped up, along with the other men but he held his hand up. "Oh no. No spectators."

"Come on, be a sport," said Frank.

"I'm not having you lot heckling me."

The men flopped back down but an exchange of glances confirmed they were all thinking the same thing. Joseph led Harry over to one of the small outbuildings and stepped inside.

"There she is, little beauty." He patted the seat affectionately.

"She's a work of art," agreed Harry. Joseph began to talk him through the basics then asked, "Where did you learn to drive?"

"At the factory where I worked with my father. I used to hang round the yard and watch the mechanics working on the delivery vans. One of the drivers started teaching me when I was fifteen."

"Does your father still work there?"

"No. He passed away a few years ago. My mother too. Where's home for you?"

"My parents live in London. My brother, Friedri…" he corrected himself. "Frederick, was killed last year, at Saint Eloi."

"Sorry to hear that," said Harry.

Joseph appeared flustered for a moment, so Harry changed the subject,

"Listen, I wondered if you could do me a favour?"

Joseph composed himself and gave Harry a questioning look. "Course, if I can. What do you need?"

Harry dug into his pocket and retrieved a cream envelope, holding it out. "Any chance you could deliver this for me?"

Joseph took the envelope and read the name, his face breaking into a smile. "And where would I find this 'Sister Davidson'?"

"No 8 Clearing Station. Thanks, Joseph."

Joseph tucked the letter into his breast pocket and said, "I'll do my best, mate. Now, let's go, shall we?"

He wheeled the motorcycle out of the door, started it up and gestured to Harry to climb on. Harry gingerly pulled the throttle, but the bike lurched and stalled. Trying again, he crept a few feet and stalled once more. On the third attempt, he pitched forward then found himself wobbling and weaving his way across the yard like a child learning to ride a bicycle, much to the delight of a jeering crowd.

"Bastards," he shouted, as he zigzagged through the gate and onto the road, Joseph and Luc chasing after him.

***

He and Joseph re-joined the group a short while later to a chorus of jibes and teasing.

"Yeh, yeh. I'd like to see you do any better." He flopped down and lit a cigarette, offering the packet around the group.

"Ignore them," said Joseph, "You did fine."

Frank snorted and Harry gave him a swipe.

Joseph blew a stream of smoke upwards. "Give him a break, lads, these roads aren't easy, as well you know."

"Reckon I could sleep for twelve hours straight," said Dev, yawning and rubbing his face.

"Wouldn't that be nice," agreed Harry. "Wonder when we'll get some leave?"

"There's something big in the pipeline," said Frank.

Harry turned to him. "Where *do* you get your information from, Frank? You never cease to amaze me."

Frank winked and tapped his nose. "I have my contacts."

"So, what's happening?" asked Joseph.

"A new offensive somewhere down the line. Fourth Army and the French."

Billy spoke up. "Could tip things in our favour apparently."

Arthur looked up and asked, "That big?"

"That big," replied Frank.

"They're sending in thousands of troops," added Billy. "Thousands."

119

"Where is this exactly?" asked Harry.

Frank looked round. "South of here. Near the River Somme."

***

The following morning, Harry crossed the camp with Luc at his heels. His ambulance had developed engine trouble the previous day and, having limped back to headquarters, was now in for repair. He was hoping he could talk whoever was working on it into allowing him to help. The barn doors were standing open, and Harry could hear whistling coming from the rear. He shouted a greeting and a face appeared. It was Reg.

"Morning," said Harry. Luc padded up to Reg, who ignored Harry's greeting and bent down to make a fuss of the dog. Harry waited patiently, accustomed to the surly Yorkshireman. Eventually, the mechanic looked up.

"Let me guess. You want to help."

Harry raised his eyebrows and grinned. Luc was sniffing Reg's overalls.

"What can you smell, lad?" He stuck his hand in his pocket and retrieved a piece of broken biscuit. Luc sat down and gave the mechanic a stare.

"Alright, it's yours." The dog wolfed down the morsel then turned his attention to exploring the barn.

"I'll do exactly as you tell me," said Harry.

"Ay, that you will," said Reg, straightening up.

"Is that a yes?" asked Harry.

"Ay, suppose so. But minute you get int' way, you're out of 'ere."

***

The two men worked steadily through the morning and just before midday Seth appeared, carrying three steaming mugs of tea. The men sat on the floor and conversation turned to Carter.

"I've never had nay bother off him," said Reg, slurping the scalding tea. Seth let out a huff. "That's 'cos he's scared of you. He knows you'd give him a pounding."

"You need to stand up to him, lad."

"Reg is right," said Harry. "Carter's a bully. And like most bullies, he's also a coward." Seth shrugged. "Easier said than done."

Harry changed the subject and turned to Reg. "Who's running the farm for you while you're here?"

"Me brother. We decided one of us would sign up and the other would take care ot' farm."

"So, you drew the short straw," said Harry.

"Well, our kid dun't see it like that." He drained his mug and wiped his mouth on his sleeve.

"Right then, Stone. Let's get this bugger back ont' road."

Seth left them to it and Luc curled up in a corner, his nosed tucked into the thick curly fur on his tail. The men worked flat out, stopping only briefly to bolt down a sandwich. They were just making final adjustments when Luc pricked up his ears.

"Convoy must be back," said Harry, gathering up the tools scattered around the floor. The sound of engines grew louder, and Luc trotted out to investigate. A moment later there was a panicked shout and Harry heard a sickening yelp. His stomach lurched. He dropped the tools and shot out of the barn. Luc was lying on his side, howling, his back leg twisted at an unnatural angle. Carter was standing by his vehicle with his hands up.

"He ran straight out in front of me."

As Harry darted over to Luc, he saw Seth hurtling towards Carter. "You did that on purpose, you bastard!"

Before Carter could protest, Seth launched at him and sent the two of them sprawling in the dirt. They grappled with each other until Seth managed to pin Carter down and started punching him in the face. Carter tried to bring his arms up to protect himself. Several of the drivers leapt from their vehicles and rushed over. It took three of them to eventually pull Seth off and drag him away. Harry knelt down next to Luc. The howling had turned to a whimper.

"It's alright, boy. It's alright." He turned and shouted, "Who's got fuel left in their car?"

Dev rushed forward. "I'll drive. You bring Luc."

Harry gently lifted Luc, while Arthur supported the injured leg. They carefully carried him to the ambulance. Dev was already behind the wheel with the engine running. As they pulled out of the yard, Harry glanced back. Lieutenant Kerr had appeared, and Seth was still hurling abuse at Carter, who was holding a handkerchief to his bleeding nose. Carter caught Harry's look and turned away, but Harry thought he saw the beginning of a smirk forming on his battered face.

Harry cradled Luc on his lap, trying his best to absorb the bumps and jolts. The dog was panting hard, his tongue hanging out of one side of his mouth. His eyes were staring, filled with panic. Night had fallen and Dev was running the gauntlet of hazards that challenged the most skilled drivers in daylight. The dirty headlights lit just a few feet of the approaching road. He peered through the windscreen into the gloom. As they headed away from the Front, conditions improved, and he managed to accelerate. Harry gave directions at each junction or fork in the road. Luc let out a whimper. His breathing had slowed right down, and his eyes had closed.

"Put your foot down," said Harry, stroking Luc's head.

Dev glanced across and could see that Luc's ribs were barely moving. He gripped the wheel and pressed on the accelerator. They hit a rut and the vehicle bounced.

"Sorry," said Dev.

Harry just carried on murmuring quietly to Luc. It was over an hour before lights appeared up ahead.

"Turn in up here, just a few yards on the left," said Harry.

Dev manoeuvred the ambulance through a gateway and pulled up next to a row of trucks. He jumped down and came round to help Harry. As they carefully lifted Luc, an officer appeared out of the darkness.

"What do we have here, gentlemen?"

"Sir, my dog. He's been hit by an ambulance car. It's his leg. I think it's broken." Without even glancing at Luc, the officer turned on his heels.

"Right. This way."

Harry and Dev followed the officer through the labyrinth of tents. The powerful smell of horses and manure pervaded the camp. He led them into a brightly lit tent lined with crates and boxes of medical supplies. He patted a scrubbed table and said, "Pop him on here."

Harry slowly laid Luc down then stepped out of the officer's way and shoved his hands in his pockets. Dev put his hand on his shoulder.

"What's his name?" asked the officer.

"Luc, Sir," said Harry, struggling to keep his voice steady.

"Right, Luc. What have you been up to, hey?"

The officer gently carried out his examination, talking quietly to Luc the whole time. Harry was aware of voices somewhere nearby and then a whinny in the distance. Eventually the officer turned to him.

"Right. We're looking at multiple fractures, including the hip. Possible internal bleeding. He would need surgery, but to be honest…" the officer paused, "I'm not sure the leg can be saved. It might be kinder to call it a day."

"No. No way." blurted Harry. "We have to try. You have to try. Please, Sir."

The officer glanced at Dev and back to Harry. "It would take up a lot of time and resources, Private. The horses are our priority."

"I know, Sir. But…" Harry's voice waivered. "He's my family." The officer stroked his chin for a moment. "Alright, Private. I'll operate. Where are you based?"

"Merville, Sir. No. 2 Convoy," replied Harry.

"I suggest you return to base, and I'll get a message to you."

"I'd prefer to stay, Sir. If that's alright." Harry looked over at Dev, who nodded.

"When are you back on duty?"

"In the morning, Sir."

"Right, I'll get someone to show you where the mess is, and you can have some tea and grub. It could be a long night."

"Thank you, Sir."

The officer disappeared and Harry gently stroked Luc. "It's going to be alright, boy."

***

Staring at the empty mug in front of him, Harry sat stewing over Carter. He was going to teach him a lesson once and for all. Dev had dozed off at the table, his head resting on folded arms. Harry heard a movement and the officer walked into the tent looking pale and tired. Dev stirred.

"Well, he's all patched up. But I can't be sure about the leg yet."

Harry took a deep breath. "Thank you, Sir, very much."

"He'll have to stay here for a few days. I'll send word when you can come and collect him. Now, get back to base and get some sleep."

The men retraced their steps back to headquarters.

"Wonder if Seth is facing any discipline," said Dev.

"The captain's a fair man," said Harry.

"Hope he broke that bastard's nose," said Dev.

"He certainly didn't hold back." Harry looked across. "Thank you."

Dev gave him a flash of his perfect teeth. "You're welcome, mate."

***

They managed to snatch a couple of hours sleep before reveille. Arthur had mumbled a sleepy enquiry about Luc when the men had crept in.

"He's going to be fine. Go back to sleep," Harry whispered.

"Seth's on a charge and Bate wants to see you and Dev first thing in the morning."

***

As soon as they were dressed, he and Dev reported to the captain's office. Bate beckoned them in and the men saluted.

"Right, Stone. I want your version of yesterday's incident and an explanation for your absence last night."

"Yes, Sir," said Harry. He described how Jones had witnessed Carter deliberately running into Luc and Dev

125

had driven him to the veterinary camp where an officer had operated. Bate sat back in his chair holding a pen between his hands. "Technically, you were both absent without leave."

"Yes, Sir," said the men.

The captain studied a document in front of him. "Your pay will be docked for one month."

"Yes, Sir."

"Dismissed." Bate began shuffling papers on his desk.

"If I may, Sir," said Harry.

"What is it?"

"I understand Private Jones has been charged, Sir."

"Yes. Disorderly conduct."

"Sir, Carter has been bullying Jones for weeks now. I think he got what he deserved."

"Private Jones' behaviour was unacceptable. And be sure both of you stay away from Carter. I will be speaking to him myself shortly."

"Yes, Sir," said Harry. The men turned to leave.

"Private Stone." Bate continued looking down at the papers. "How's the dog?"

"He should be fine, thank you, Sir."

The men left the office and made their way to breakfast. As soon as they entered, Harry spotted Carter in the far corner. One of his eyes was bruised and half closed. His lips were cut and swollen, and his nose looked misshapen. Seth had done a good job. The chatter stopped and Carter looked up, visibly tensing. Harry stared at him until he lowered his eyes.

"How's Luc?" said Frank.

"He should be fine. Fractured leg and hip. He's at the veterinary camp for a few days."

When Harry glanced back over, Carter had slunk away.

Chapter Eighteen

It was late November and Rose lay in her bunk watching her breath form a swirling, white cloud above her. She peeled off a glove and touched the end of her nose. It was as cold as ice, and she rubbed it to get some feeling back. Despite wearing a woollen hat, gloves, socks, and a cardigan in addition to her nightshirt, she had woken repeatedly with the chill seeping into her. She had to get a move on but dreaded the thought of climbing out of bed. Picturing a mug of tea waiting for her and bracing herself for the cold, she leapt up and whipped off her night attire. Jumping up and down on the spot, she grabbed her uniform and dressed in record time. She threw on her coat, and hurried to breakfast, making a short detour to relieve herself and splash water on her face.

The mess was noisy and smoky as usual, but more importantly it was warm. She joined the queue and a few minutes later was sitting clutching her tea with a plate of bread and jam in front of her. Her fellow diners were three despatch riders swapping stories. Their uniforms were splattered with mud, and each had a pair of goggles hanging loosely round his neck. They had stuffed their long leather gloves into upturned caps, lying on the table. One of them was a fresh-faced young man with a thick Scottish brogue.

"I'd parked my motorcycle outside a café in Boulogne and when I came out a group of French lassies had decorated it with flowers and garlands. They even wanted to put a flower in my cap!"

Rose sipped her tea and smiled at the image. Another rider spoke up. "I nearly didn't make it onto the train at Victoria. We decided to take the motorcycles for a spin up and down the platform. Terrific fun. But the guard was furious and wanted us all charged."

The men laughed and continued eating. Rose took a bite of the sticky bread. She had the sense she was being watched and looked across the rows of tables. A man was studying her intently and when he saw her look over, he winked then continued to stare. She felt her colour rise and lowered her gaze. Something about him sent a shiver down her spine and made her shift uncomfortably in her seat. She gulped her tea and slapped the bread and jam together to make a sandwich she could take with her. As she stood, she stole a glance over the tables but to her relief the man had gone. Wrapping her coat around her, she ventured out into the freezing air. She'd taken just a few steps when a figure stepped into her path. They almost collided and Rose dropped the sandwich. It was him.

"Hello there, beautiful."

"Good morning." Rose retrieved her sandwich and made to move on, but the man blocked her way. "Where are you going in such a hurry?"

"I'm on duty shortly, if you'll excuse me."

"Well, perhaps when you're not on duty, we could get together sometime? My name's Edward." He reached out and rubbed Rose's arm, a thin smile on his face. Rose instinctively backed away and his smile vanished. "Don't be like that. I saw you looking at me."

Rose started to protest then realised it would be futile. "I'm sorry, I must be going." She darted round him and quickened her pace, half expecting him to grab her, but instead, she heard him call after her. "See you again soon, Rose."

Her head spun round. "How do you know my...?"

But the man was walking away in the opposite direction.

***

The encounter shook Rose and it played on her mind for the rest of the day. She hadn't once felt that sort of unease since arriving in France. The patients, orderlies and medical officers had shown her nothing but courtesy and respect. She tried to concentrate on her work and block it from her mind. Hopefully their paths would never cross again.

Chapter Nineteen

As Harry peered through the window, his warm breath instantly misted up the glass. He rubbed it away and surveyed the glistening white world outside. The mud in the yard was frozen hard, the ruts now permanently marked with tyre tracks and edged with sharp ridges. The fields beyond the farm buildings had a blanket of twinkling frost. Joseph was just leaving, and Harry silently thanked him for carrying another letter to Rose.

He heard someone attempting to start one of the vehicles, the engine struggling to fight the cold. The plummeting temperatures were wreaking havoc with the cars, and it was a continual battle to keep them running. The mechanics had been waking through the night to turn the engines over every half an hour to prevent them from freezing up.

Luc hopped off Harry's bed and made a beeline for Arthur, treating him to a wet muzzle. Whilst he had been recovering from his injury, Luc had been permitted to sleep indoors and now winter had arrived, he remained in the billet with the men. He trotted over to Dev and nudged his snout under the covers, prompting mumbling from beneath the covers. The other drivers were stirring, bracing themselves for the painful process of dressing in the icy air.

As they filed through to breakfast, Harry noticed Carter taking a seat just a couple of chairs along. Usually, the two men preferred to give each other a wide berth. Within minutes, Carter's booming voice could be heard above the general chatter.

"Met the most adorable nurse yesterday at No.8 Station. Pretty little filly, she was. Caught her staring at me." Harry and Arthur exchanged looks and Frank rolled his eyes. Carter continued, casting a glance down the table. "She had the most remarkable blue eyes."

Harry froze.

"We had a little chat and a bit of a flirt. 'Rose', I think she was called."

In an instant, Harry felt his contempt for Carter transform into rage and he sprang from his seat, sending mugs and plates flying. He hurled himself at Carter, who landed heavily on his back. Grabbing Carter's collar, he yanked him up, so their faces were inches apart. "You stay away from her," he snarled.

"I didn't realise you knew her, Stone," said Carter, smirking.

"Just keep away from her, do you hear?"

"Steady on, old boy. It's a free world. And I must say, she couldn't keep her hands off me."

Harry's fist hit Carter square on the nose. There was a sickening crunch and blood poured down his face. Arthur and Frank had leapt up and now they grabbed Harry's shoulders and pulled him off before he could land another punch.

"I'm warning you," yelled Harry, as the two men manhandled him out of the door and into the yard.

"For God's sake, you'll be put on a charge," said Arthur.

"You heard him. He's going after Rose."

"He's just trying to rile you."

"Yeah well, it worked." Harry stretched his hand and rubbed his knuckles. "Bastard." Captain Bate appeared in the doorway, eyes blazing. "Private Stone. My office this instant."

Arthur gave Harry a wry look and said, "I'll save you some breakfast."

***

131

Moments later, Harry stood in front of Bate's desk. The captain was shuffling papers and slamming drawers. He finally looked up. "Listen to me, Private. I will not have disorderly conduct in my unit, do you understand?"

"Yes, Sir."

"If you and Private Carter don't see eye to eye then stay away from each other."

"Yes, Sir."

"This is the second time I've had to speak to you. Extra latrine duties for seven days. If this happens again, you will be on a charge, Private. Understood?"

"Yes, Sir."

"Dismissed."

Harry saluted and retreated out the door, relieved the punishment hadn't been more severe. Now he had a new worry. Rose surely couldn't be interested in Carter, could she?

***

The freezing temperatures and snowy conditions continued, bringing with them an increasing number of cases of frostbite. Harry and the other drivers sensed a shift in the mood of the soldiers coming from the Front and as the icy weather persisted, it was clear morale was dropping. On a bitter morning in mid-January, the drivers came into the yard to find the mechanics huddled around drawings spread across an ambulance bonnet.

"What's going on?" asked Arthur, peering over their shoulders.

"Plans for heating the cars," replied Reg.

"To try and keep the casualties a bit warmer," added Seth.

Harry's interest was piqued. "How're they going to do that?"

Seth turned sideways to let Harry get a glimpse of the plans. "Quite clever, really. Divert the hot exhaust gases through pipes running along the walls in the back of the cars."

"Simple but ingenious," agreed Arthur. "Can they run through the cab too, to keep us drivers warm?"

The group of mechanics turned round to him as one. Arthur held his hands up. "Just asking."

"Looks like we'll be working through the night again, lads," said Reg, folding up the plans. "Let's get cracking."

***

It was a cold morning at the end of January and Harry was waiting in a row of cars parked outside Merville train station, as stretchers were unloaded for transfer to a train destined for Boulogne. He had listened to the soldiers in the back of his car, laughing and joking. The sense of relief at heading home was palpable. It was one of the nicer trips he had made.

"Give my regards to Blighty, lads," he called, as the men were carried away. He untied the canvas flaps and let them drop down. There seemed to be a hold up at the front of the line, so he pulled a pack of cigarettes from his pocket. He was just lighting up when he heard a voice calling and turning, he saw a nurse with blonde curls and carrying a small case, striding towards him. It took him a moment to realise it was Amy.

"I'm so happy to see you," she said.

"Amy! Where are you off to?"

"Bailleul. No.8 Station. Just waiting for a lift."

"Ah, you'll see Rose, then," said Harry, offering her a cigarette. She looked up at him in surprise. "Rose is at No. 8?"

133

"Since April last year. No. 2 Station was bombed."

"Oh God. Was she hurt?"

"Nasty cut and burns to her hand but she's recovered well."

"So, you've seen her...?" Amy raised her eyebrows. Harry declined to answer and just smiled. She rolled her eyes at his discretion. "I can't believe I'm going to see Rose again. Any message you'd like me to pass on?" she asked mischievously.

Harry looked serious. "Actually, yes. Can you tell her to watch out for a driver called Carter. Edward Carter."

A look of concern crossed her face. "What's going on?"

"He's got an axe to grind with me and I'm worried he's going to involve Rose. He's a nasty piece of work."

There was a blast of horns from behind and Harry realised the vehicles in front had moved off. He climbed into the cab. "Oh and tell her my cap still smells of lavender."

***

He returned to headquarters to see a waggon parked up with a figure sitting hunched in the back and two military policemen standing guard. Arthur and the other drivers were loitering by the workshops, smoking, and kicking dirt around with their hands in their pockets. Harry strode over. "What's going on?"

"It's Joseph," said Billy.

The men looked at each other and Arthur moved to his side. "He's been caught spying."

Harry's mouth gaped open. "Spying? That can't be right."

"He's been working with the butcher in La Couture. They were caught communicating with the Germans. The butcher's been executed."

"But why would Joseph help them? It doesn't make sense."

Arthur shrugged. Harry scanned the faces around him then glanced across at the waggon. "I'm going to speak to him."

"That's not a good idea, mate," said Dev, but Harry ignored him and marched across the yard. As he approached, the guards blocked his path.

"Back off, Private."

"Just five minutes."

"Against regulations."

"Come on. He's my mate."

"I wouldn't be saying that too loudly, if I were you."

"Please."

The men exchanged a look and stepped aside. "Make it quick."

Joseph was handcuffed and sitting with his head hanging down. Harry clambered up and perched on the opposite bench. "Is it true?" There was no reply. "Joseph. Is it true?"

Joseph lifted his head and Harry recoiled from the look of venom in his eyes. "Yes, it's true," he said.

Harry studied his features, twisted and ugly with rage. "But why?"

Joseph shifted position and gazed out of the back of the waggon. After a few moments he spoke. "My mother is German. When war broke out, she was devastated. My brother and I decided to fight for England. We'd been born in London and grew up there. My mother understood but she found it hard. Friedrich joined the infantry using the name Frederick and was sent to the Front." He paused. "He was in some woods with a scouting party, and they came across enemy soldiers. There was a skirmish and Friedrich got separated. He was disorientated and couldn't work out which direction to go to get back to the Allied line. So, he dug in and hid. When he was eventually found, he was accused of deserting."

Harry sat back, absorbing the information. Joseph's face was distorted with pain and anger. "They executed him." He leant forward and snarled into Harry's face. "The British Army shot him like a dog." He slumped back and dropped his head. One of the military policemen appeared.

"Time's up."

Harry jumped down without saying a word and took a final look at his friend. Joseph had resumed his hunched position. Captain Bate appeared with a third military policeman, who signalled to his men they were leaving. Harry re-joined the group, and they watched in silence as Joseph was driven away.

Chapter Twenty

Rose was tending to a patient when she heard a familiar voice behind her.

"Bonjour, mon amie."

She turned to see her best friend standing before her, an excited grin lighting up her face. "Amy!" She rushed forward and the women embraced.

"Are you stationed here now?" asked Rose.

"Yes. We're going to be together again."

"Where have you been working. Tell me everything."

"I will. I will. But first I want to hear about you and Harry."

"Harry? What do you mean?"

"Well, you are together now, aren't you?"

Rose stepped back in astonishment. "How on earth do you know that?"

"I bumped into him at Merville train station."

"And he told you?" asked Rose.

"Well, not in so many words, but it was obvious."

Rose shook her head and smiled. "I've missed you."

"And I've missed you. Now when do you finish your shift so we can have a proper catchup?"

"Five o'clock. We can have supper together."

Amy picked up her case and turned to leave. "By the way, Harry said to tell you to beware of a chap called Carter. Do you know him?"

It only took a moment for Rose to realise who Harry was talking about. "Yes, I know him."

***

The following morning Rose emerged from her tent to find everywhere under a mantle of thick snow. As she gazed across the fields, the sun glistened on the white blanket as far as the eye could see, creating a wonderland she had previously never witnessed. City living didn't offer the kind of panoramic vista laid out before her and it took her breath away.

She became aware of icy water seeping into her boots. Time to move. Orderlies were labouring with shovels to clear paths through the camp, creating piles of snow every few yards, as if giant moles had been at work overnight. She picked her way around them and made her way to the Moribund tent. Her shifts here were long and demanding, trying to comfort those patients deemed to have no chance of surviving their injuries. Some lingered for days, others just hours. But she tackled the work with as much devotion and care as any other posting.

As she entered, she saw the chaplain leaning over a soldier, a nurse kneeling beside him holding the boy's hand. Rose paused and listened to the hushed murmurs of the last rites. She lowered her head and waited. Within minutes the nurse was gently closing the soldier's eyes and pulling the sheet over his young face. Rose sighed and crossed to the nurses' station, greeting the sisters already on duty. Some of the patients were babbling and writhing with fever, their shirts and covers damp with sweat. Others were quiet and still, waiting for the last breath to take them to pain-free oblivion.

A minute later, the chaplain approached. He was tall and slim and had an athleticism that belied his years. Rose had found him to be unexpectedly witty and charming with a talent for storytelling, characteristics she was surprised to find in a man of the cloth. His entertaining anecdotes were never inappropriate nor ill-timed but rather the perfect tonic for the bleak and joyless work they were carrying out.

"Good morning, Sister."

"Good morning, Padre."

"Not the best start to the day."

"It never ends, Sir."

"Indeed."

The chaplain was lost in his thoughts for a moment, then spoke. "I'm on a tea round. Would you like one?"

"Yes please, Sir."

"I'll see if I can rustle up some biscuits for us all."

"Lovely, thank you, Sir."

He put on his cap and headed off. Rose looked over at the deceased soldier and realised the nurse was still on her knees at his bedside. She approached and the nurse quickly wiped her eyes. Rose patted her shoulder. "Would you like some help?"

The woman gave a sniff and nodded. "I'm sorry."

"It's alright. Why don't you go and find the orderlies and ask them to bring a stretcher?"

"Yes. Thank you."

The nurse hurried away, and Rose knelt. She drew back the sheet and revealed the cord holding two identity discs resting around the soldier's neck. She carefully removed the green, octagonal disc and studied it for a moment. The soldiers called it a 'cold meat ticket' but Rose had always hated the term. The circular one was left in place, where it would remain for ever. She checked for any personal belongings that could be forwarded to the grieving family and then replaced the covers. Returning to the desk, she recorded the death, transposing the details from the disc to the ledger.

By the time she finished, the nurse had returned with two stretcher bearers, closely followed by the chaplain carrying a tray of mugs. His coat was peppered with wet snow and his cap was tipped forward, slightly obscuring his view.

"Are you alright, Padre?" asked Rose.

"Some chaps having a snowball fight. Thought it

would be jolly funny to use me as target practice."

Rose tried to hide her smile. The chaplain placed the tray on the desk and grabbed a biscuit, adding with a grin, "Didn't spill a drop, though, did I?"

***

Finally, Harry found himself at No 8 Station and was desperate to seek Rose out. He and Arthur were travelling together while Arthur's car was having minor repair work.

"I'm just going to say a quick hello to Rose. See you in ten minutes."

Arthur had spotted a group of patients playing cards and was already heading in their direction. "Take as long as you like," he called.

Harry made his way through the camp, but a minute later, he stopped in his tracks. Ten yards up ahead, Rose was deep in conversation with a soldier, an infantryman, his rifle slung over his shoulder. Harry moved out of sight and watched the exchange. Both had serious expressions on their faces. The soldier was holding a posy of flowers which he offered to Rose and as she took them, he leant forward and gave her a peck on the cheek. Harry felt a rush of jealousy. He watched the two of them embrace and in that moment his heart began to break.

Turning on his heels, he stormed back to the car, hurt, and confused. Had Rose fallen for someone else? Had she not meant anything she said? He reached the ambulance and yelled over to Arthur, "We're leaving."

Arthur snatched up his winnings and trotted over. "Did you find her, then?"

"Just get in," snapped Harry, clambering into the cab.

"Alright, keep your hair on. What's happened?"

"Turns out, it wasn't Carter I should have been

140

worried about."

Arthur frowned. "Not following you."

"Forget it." Harry slammed his foot down sending the car fishtailing its way out of the field, Arthur gripping the dashboard with one hand and Luc with the other.

***

The cold weather hung on throughout February and into March. Amy had quickly settled in and successfully charmed the male population of No.8 Station. Her wish was their command and Rose continually marvelled at the items that once again began to magically appear, from extra blankets and hot water bottles to delicious chocolate and creamy French cheese. Amy's exuberance and zest for life gave all who encountered her a shot of much-needed joy and Rose felt grateful for the luck that had brought her friend back to her.

But she missed Harry and couldn't understand why he hadn't been to visit her, and why the letters had stopped. She worried that he was injured, but having bumped into other members of No2 Convoy, she had been assured he was well. All she could do was concentrate on her work and hope that he would appear one day soon.

***

By mid-March the first signs of spring were appearing, and she finally had a day off. She contemplated hitching a lift to Merville and going in search of Harry, but she couldn't bear the thought of a cold reception from him. Instead, she made plans for a walk and picnic in the woods, hoping Amy would join her, and put the idea to her over supper.

"Sorry, Rose. I'm on shift tomorrow."

"Can't you swap with someone?"

"I've already swapped once. Don't think Sister will be too happy if I do it again."

Rose sunk back in her seat. "I'll just have to go on my own then."

"You'll enjoy the peace and quiet."

"I suppose. A bit of time to myself might be quite nice."

***

The following afternoon, she was sitting on the ground watching a blackbird hopping between the dangling snowdrops, pecking here and there. She held herself still, not wanting to frighten him. The carpet of white flowers stretched into the wood as far she could see. The trees were still mostly bare, with just a few tiny buds appearing, heralding the forthcoming spring.

There was a rustle in the undergrowth and the bird took flight. Rose leant back against the tree and closed her eyes. She didn't care that the cold from the earth was creeping into her legs and back. All she could hear was birdsong. She loved the plants that bravely flowered first, when the ground was still hard, and snow often lingered. And the fragile blossom that would inevitably be swept from the trees by the March winds. As she sat there, the war felt distant and unreal. She thought about her parents back at home. Her father had been unwell, but it was hard to tell how serious his illness was. Her mother's letter had skimmed over the matter and Rose suspected she was trying to protect her in some way. If anything, it made her worry more.

The wind suddenly lifted, and she shivered. Time to make a move. She pulled her coat around her and put on her straw boater, securing it with a long hat pin. Standing up, she brushed herself down and gathered up the remains of lunch, stowing them in the canvas knapsack slung across her shoulder. She meandered back through the trees in the direction of the road. She had persuaded one of the drivers from the Army Service Corps to make a slight detour from his supply run and drop her on the edge of the woods. He promised to pick her up on his return trip. She emerged from the wood and perched on a fallen tree, the bark having flaked off long ago and the trunk the colour of driftwood, bleached by winter winds and summer sun.

Fifteen minutes later, she caught the rumble of an engine and stood up to wave. But as the vehicle drew nearer, she realised it wasn't the truck but rather an ambulance. And the driver looked horribly familiar.

***

Carter had spotted the lone figure in the distance and once he realised it was female, he had every intention of stopping to see if he could be of service to this potential damsel in distress. When Rose's face came into view, he couldn't believe his eyes. Or his luck.

Rose had dropped her arm and stepped back from the road. What on earth was he doing here? As the car pulled up, she could feel her heart pounding. Carter flashed her a lewd smile as he stepped out of the cab. "Well, well, well, Rose. What are you doing out here in the middle of nowhere? All alone."

"Just taking a walk. My lift will be here any moment." Rose glanced up the road willing the truck to appear. Carter offered her a cigarette. When she shook her head, he lit one for himself and stared intently at her. "I can give you a lift if you like."

"No, thank you. I'd better stick to the arrangements."

He took a step towards her. Rose pulled her coat around her and edged back. Despite the cold, a trickle of sweat was working its way down her back. Her mind was racing. Instinct told her she was in trouble. She looked up the road again, hoping to see a vehicle, but it was still empty. As she took another step back her heel hit the tree trunk and suddenly she was off balance and tipping backwards. Carter lunged forward and caught her.

"I've got you." He pulled her close to him and she could smell a mixture of cigarettes and sour breath.

"Thank you." She tried to move away but Carter held his grip.

"You were nearly flat on your back there," he said.

She could feel panic rising and for the first time in her life, real fear. She felt Carter's hand slip inside her coat, and he bent to kiss her. She turned her face away and struggled against his grasp. "Let go of me."

Carter tightened his hold. "Don't be like that. I know you like me, Rose."

"I don't. I don't like you. Get off me."

His face darkened and as he released his grip he gave her a shove, sending her sprawling backwards over the tree trunk. The fall winded her and she lay dazed for a moment, but Carter had hurdled the tree and was now on top of her, pulling at her skirt. She went to scratch his face, but he grabbed her arms and pinned them above her head. Tears were streaming down her face as she realised, she was helpless. His face was heavy with lust, his eyes glazed. As Rose squirmed and writhed beneath him, she felt his grip on her arms loosen for an instant and she took the chance to free her right hand. She needed a weapon. And then it came to her. She snatched at the pin still holding her hat to her hair and stabbed at Carter's cheek. He howled in pain, and she stabbed again. Carter rolled away clutching his face, blood pouring between his fingers. Rose scrabbled to her feet and sprinted towards the road. She thought she heard a vehicle and sure enough, trundling down the road was her lift. She continued running, not daring to look behind her. She clambered aboard, ignoring the driver's shocked expression.

"Drive! Please, drive," she cried. As the truck pulled away, she saw Carter holding a blood-stained handkerchief to his cheek, staring at her with pure venom. She was shaking uncontrollably and began to sob. The driver was at a loss as to what to do. He attempted a few diplomatic questions but soon realised she was unwilling to talk, and he concentrated on the road, trying to ignore the sound of Rose's tears filling the cab.

By the time they arrived at the clearing station, Rose had summoned all her energy and will power to compose herself. She dried her eyes and rearranged her clothing. Her hat had been lost so she tidied her hair as best she could and tweaked it back into a bun. She hoped no one would notice the dirt staining her skirt and jacket. She thanked the driver and apologised for her behaviour. Dashing to her tent, she swiftly changed out of her clothes and into uniform. Work was the only thing to block out the horrors of the afternoon. Bruising was appearing on her wrists, and she pulled her cuffs down as far as possible.

The Senior Sister looked up in surprise when Rose entered the tent and Amy gave her a puzzled stare from across the rows of beds.

"You're not on duty today, Davidson," said the sister.

"I know, Sister, but the ward is full and thought you might need an extra pair of hands."

The woman studied her for a moment. "Is everything alright?"

"Yes, thank you, Sister. What would you like me to

do?"

"Could you change the sheets of the patient in the far corner, please." She watched Rose zigzag round the bunks, not convinced all was well.

Rose set to work but within a minute, Amy was by her side. "What are you doing here?" she whispered.

"Just thought I'd help," replied Rose, avoiding Amy's gaze.

"What's wrong? What's happened?"

"Nothing. I knew you were shorthanded, that's all." She knew Amy wasn't fooled.

"Something's wrong, I can tell," said Amy.

"Oh, for goodness sake, Amy. Leave me alone and get on with your work."

Amy recoiled in shock and her eyes immediately filled with tears. She backed away and retreated across the tent. Rose busied herself, cursing the way she'd snapped at her friend. But she had to stop the questioning. Eventually, she would have folded.

She worked through the night, not being able to bear the thought of lying in the dark and re-living the assault. She and Amy skirted round each other, and Rose noticed, when Amy's shift was over, she left without saying goodbye. It was nearing midnight when the duty sister ordered her to go to bed.

"I understand you're doing a voluntary shift, Davidson, but everything's under control and you look exhausted. Get yourself off." Rose was about to protest but the sister continued, "As commendable as it is, you're no good to us if you make yourself ill."

She nodded and a minute later, stepped out into a clear night, pausing to take a deep breath of the cold, cleansing air. The camp was quiet with just the odd person moving about. She suddenly felt uneasy and scanned around her, half expecting Carter to loom at her from the shadows.

She hurried to her quarters, glancing over her shoulder every few moments, and ducked into her tent, breathless and perspiring. Amy was tucked up in her bunk, deep under the covers. Rose sat down, trying to calm her breathing. She fought back the tears.

"Are you going to tell me what happened?"

She jumped at the sound of Amy's voice.

"Look at the state of you? What is going on?"

Rose couldn't hold back the tears any longer and covered her face with her hands. Amy wrapped herself in her sheet and moved across to sit beside her. Rose sunk into her friend's arms and sobbed. After a couple of minutes, she managed to say, "I'm sorry I snapped at you."

"I know. It's alright. Just tell me what happened."

Rose talked and Amy listened. They huddled together through the night and Amy whispered words of comfort until the early hours.

Chapter Twenty-one

Torrential rain lashed against the windscreen, obliterating Harry's view. The wipers were having little effect and twice he had nearly shunted into the vehicle in front as it loomed into view. The roads had once again become no more than muddy tracks. His car suddenly lurched sideways and he gripped the wheel as he manoeuvred out of the shimmy. Through the downpour, he could see a group of soldiers battling to free two horses and the artillery gun they were hauling, out of the bog. The horses were already up to their flanks, their heads flailing in panic. Harry could see their eyes, wide with fear, as they fought to escape the thick sludge. Ropes had been lassoed round their necks and the men were heaving with all their strength. Come on, come on. But their efforts were in vain and as the last visible part of the gun vanished into the slime, the terrified horses were dragged with it. Harry looked away. It didn't matter how many times he witnessed scenes like that, they still shook him.

A short time later, he pulled up in front of a two-storey building, once a school. Every window was shattered, and the brickwork was peppered with shell damage. Now a main dressing station, the queue of ambulance cars stretched the length of the building. Through the deluge, he caught sight of Carter, a large dressing covering his left cheek. He was pretty sure Carter deserved whatever had been inflicted on him.

As the last casualty was offloaded, he heard his name and turned to see Arthur approaching. "We've been ordered back to the Front," he said.

"What do you mean?" asked Harry, throwing a pile of damp and dirty blankets in the back of the car.

"There's some wounded still at the advanced dressing station, just south of Passchendaele."

"I thought everyone was evacuated."

"Apparently not. I'll park my car and we'll go together." He pulled up the collar of his coat and disappeared into the torrent.

Harry climbed back into his vehicle and shook off the wet. His saturated uniform clung to him as if it had shrunk two sizes. Luc wagged his tail and gave Harry's knee a nudge, then settled back down in the foot well. As he waited for Arthur, Harry caught a flash in the sky out of the corner of his eye, followed a moment later by a loud thunderclap. Arthur appeared and climbed into the cab. "That's all we need, a thunderstorm."

"All adds to the fun," said Harry.

***

It took almost an hour to reach the abandoned station. They had driven towards the storm and against the flow of horses and retreating soldiers, until eventually the route was deserted. Ahead of him, Harry could see the road dipped and was submerged beneath a fast-moving stream of water. He slowed to walking pace and eased through the flow. The level was rising by the minute.

"I don't think we're going to get back across this," said Arthur, leaning out of the cab to see how far up the wheels the water was reaching. Harry grimaced. The car skidded slightly but made it out the other side and a minute later, they pulled up outside a stone barn sitting by the side of the road. Surprisingly, the structure had suffered little damage. The roof was intact, and the walls appeared sound.

Harry instructed Luc to stay, and he and Arthur made a dash for the door. A medical officer was kneeling in between two stretchers on the far side of the barn and jumped up in surprise as the two men entered. He was momentarily dazed then stepped forward to greet them.

"Bloody good to see you, gentlemen. I didn't think anyone was coming for us." He wiped a hand across his brow, relief evident on his face. "I've got two casualties with chest injuries, both needing surgery."

Harry and Arthur exchanged a look. "Sorry, Sir, but we can't get back at the moment. The road's underwater. We only just got through," said Arthur.

The officer ran his hand through his hair and glanced back at his patients. "Right, well, just have to do what I can for them." He turned back and continued, "But we have another problem, gentlemen. The enemy. They'll be sending a clearing party through, now we've retreated. I've been expecting them for a couple of hours."

The three of them stood in grim silence.

"Do you have any weapons?" asked the officer.

"No, Sir. We're both just drivers," said Harry.

"Right, no weapons. Well, let's hope the weather deters them for now."

A crash of thunder boomed overhead, and the men jumped.

"Should we bring the car into the barn, out of sight?" asked Arthur.

"I don't think there's any point. They know it's a dressing station. They had searchlights sweeping round last night so their snipers could take some pot shots."

One of the wounded men groaned and the officer moved across to tend to him. "We'll just have to hole up for the night and pray the water subsides before the Germans advance."

"I'll get the blankets from the car and bring Luc in," said Arthur.

The barn was falling into gloom as daylight faded. Harry eyed the detritus littering the floor. Blood-soaked dressings and bandages lay amongst a carpet of wrappers, discarded in the rush to save lives. He recognised the familiar branding of the manufacturer, *S. Maw, Son & Sons*. Three stained treatment tables stood abandoned in the middle of the barn. He approached the stretchers. "Anything I can do, Sir?" he asked.

"They're stable for now. Just need to keep them warm."

"Arthur...I mean Private Richards is fetching blankets, Sir," said Harry.

"What's your name, Private?"

"Stone, Sir."

"Major Bradley."

"Pleasure, Sir."

The barn door creaked, and Luc trotted towards him, followed by Arthur with an armful of blankets.

"And who's this fella?" asked the Major.

"Luc, Sir," replied Harry.

Luc began a scout of the barn, nose to the floor. Arthur offered two blankets to Bradley for the casualties, then set to clearing the litter to make space for the three of them to rest. He was surprised to see a small pile of clean straw in the corner of the barn. He scattered it across the cleared floor and lay the blankets on top. The Major came over to join them.

"I've given them morphine, but I'll need to watch them." He accepted the cigarette Harry was holding out and leant forward for the light. He had discarded his tunic and rolled up the sleeves of his undershirt. Barely an inch of clothing wasn't stained, and large rings of sweat had spread from his armpits. He dropped onto the blankets and leant against the wall, eyes closed. Harry and Arthur sat down alongside him, and Luc squeezed in between.

"How long have you been in the war, Private?" asked Bradley.

"Two years, Sir," replied Harry. "We met at training

in Aldershot."

"Didn't think I'd still be stuck with him," said Arthur.

Bradley smiled and took a draw on his cigarette. "Which convoy are you with?"

"No. 2, Sir, based in Merville."

"Anyone waiting at home for you, Stone?"

Harry hesitated. "No, Sir. But Private Richards here has a whole tribe."

"Oh, yes?"

"Yes, Sir. Six little angels," replied Arthur. "How about you, Sir?"

"A wife and son." The officer dug into his pocket and pulled out a folded photograph, handing it over. "Hardest thing in the world to say goodbye to them."

"Most definitely, Sir," agreed Arthur, returning the photograph, and offering his family picture for Bradley to see.

"You have been busy, Private," said the Major, smiling at the image.

The men sat listening to the rain drumming on the roof. The thunder appeared to have passed over, but they could hear it rolling round in the distance. Bradley yawned loudly.

"Why don't you grab some kip, Sir?" said Harry. "We'll keep an eye on the casualties."

The officer looked across at to the stretchers, clearly tempted by the offer. "Maybe just half an hour. But wake me immediately if there's any change."

"Course, Sir."

The Major heaved himself up and moved across to check on his patients, returning a few moments later with his tunic. He lay it over himself as he stretched out and within minutes was snoring peacefully.

Arthur lit another cigarette and passed one to Harry. He blew out a long stream of smoke and cast a look around the barn, taking in the blood-stained debris and the two wounded soldiers.

"I never wanted to enlist you know?" he said quietly.

Harry turned his head in surprise.

"Flo convinced me. It was my duty, she said." Arthur shook his head. "But I couldn't bear the thought of leaving the little 'uns."

Harry didn't speak.

"I couldn't understand why she was so keen for me to leave. Why would she want me to go to war? Turns out she was getting comments. Snide remarks. People muttering under their breath. Arthur too scared to volunteer, is he? All the other menfolk are fighting. Your husband a coward? And then we got a white feather through the letterbox."

He lifted his head and looked directly at Harry. "I'm no coward."

Harry placed his hand on his friend's shoulder. "I know, mate."

The thunder appeared to be returning and Luc whimpered.

"It's alright, boy," said Harry, flicking ash from his cigarette. He took a deep breath and then murmured, "I was married."

It was Arthur's turn to look round in surprise. Harry continued. "We were childhood sweethearts. There was never anyone else. It was always Mary." He took a long drag on his cigarette. "She fell pregnant soon after we got married. She was so excited. We both were. I'd taken an extra shift at work. Trying to earn as much as possible, you know?"

Arthur waited.

"We hadn't seen a lot of each other, I'd been working so much. She begged me not to go that day. She was about eight months gone and she'd had a twinge that morning, but she said it was nothing. Anyway, I went…" His voice trailed off. "A neighbour heard her screaming. They sent for the doctor but by the time he arrived it was too late for Mary. And the baby. A haemorrhage, he said." He wiped a tear from the corner of his eye. "It was a boy."

Arthur touched his arm, struggling to find the right words.

"I should've been there," said Harry. "Simple as that. I should've been there, and I wasn't."

"It wasn't your fault. You do know that?"

Harry shook his head. Arthur shifted position so he was facing his friend. "Now you listen to me. Tragedies happen and that was a tragedy of the worst kind. God knows, I can't imagine what I would do if I lost Flo or one of the little 'uns." He paused. "From the day we met, I knew you were hurting and now I understand why. Of all the horrors we witness every day, I see that's the thing that still hurts you the most."

Harry wiped away another tear. Luc had roused and was watching him intently.

"But Rose is your way forward, Harry. You can have a future with her. Not the one you thought you were going to have, but a happy future none the less. Rose can help you mend."

Harry gave him a weak smile. "Problem is, I saw her with someone else."

"So what? Are you really going to let that stop you? When we get out of here, go and find her. Find out once and for all. You owe it to yourself."

The two friends sat smoking while the thunder rumbled around them.

***

The Major slept for an hour before one of the casualties stirred and Harry woke him. As the hours passed, the rain eased and eventually stopped, leaving just the sound of water dripping. There was an eerie silence as dawn approached. Arthur left the barn to check on the water level, reappearing a moment later. "It's dropped. I think we could get through."

"Right," said Bradley, "Let's load the casualties and get moving. We're on borrowed time here."

Harry and Arthur ferried the first stretcher to the car while the Major gathered the blankets and joined them by the ambulance. Luc suddenly began to growl, and the men turned to see movement in the distance, black smudges in the murk of first light.

"Get the car started, Stone," said the Major, a sense of urgency in his tone. "We'll fetch the other stretcher."

Harry jumped into the cab, Luc behind him, and turned the ignition. He watched the two men emerge from the barn, struggling in the mud with the heavy load.

"C'mon. C'mon," he muttered.

"I'll go in the back," said Bradley to Arthur, hauling himself in beside his patients.

"Yes, Sir."

Arthur leapt into the cab and took a glance back. The smudges were now distinct figures, and they were moving fast. "Better get a move on, my friend."

Harry pressed the accelerator, but the wheels just spun in the mud. "For crying out loud." He slammed the lever into reverse and tried again. The engine revved. He saw out of the corner of his eye, Bradley had jumped back out of the car and was pointing at a pile of wood stacked against the barn wall. "I'll lay a plank in front of each wheel," he called.

"I'll help him," said Arthur.

Harry waited for what seemed an eternity, his heart

thumping in his chest. He heard a shout.

"Try now."

He pushed the pedal and felt the tyres grip. The car eased forward. "Get in! Get in!" he yelled.

Arthur was helping Bradley to clamber back up when he heard the unmistakable crack of gunfire and both men jumped. More shots rang out and Arthur watched in horror as the Major slumped forward then slid back down onto the ground, his head a mass of blood and shattered bone. He ran round to the cab and flung himself in. "Go! Go!" he roared.

Harry put his foot down and the car lurched forward. He could hear bullets pinging off the back of the vehicle. Pressing the pedal hard to the floor, they reached the ford in a matter of moments and then he had no option but to slow down. A volley of shots rang out. They came out the other side and he accelerated away. Arthur clung to his seat and tried to wedge Luc with his knees as the ambulance bounced and skidded along. They'd covered a mile when he risked a glance out of the cab. The barn was now just a small block in the distance and the gunfire had stopped.

"You can ease off. We're clear."

Harry slowed right down and wiped the sweat from his brow. He gave Luc a pat. "We made it, boy." He glanced sideways at Arthur. "That was a bit close for comfort, hey?"

Arthur didn't answer.

"You alright?" asked Harry.

"The Major didn't make it."

Harry stared ahead in stunned silence. For the rest of the journey, all he could think about was the Major's wife and son.

***

Harry lay awake that night, images flashing through his head. The Major, his skull obliterated. Rose, in the arms of another man. Mary, bleeding and alone. Arthur's words of advice repeated over and over until he decided what to do.

At the first opportunity, he went in search of Rose. As he approached the clearing station, a convoy of trucks and ambulances passed him moving in the opposite direction. He continued and, as more vehicles rolled by, he realised with a sinking feeling, what was happening. He pulled to a stop and gaped at the scene before him. The field had been stripped bare and was now a patchwork of yellow rectangles and circles where wards, theatres and accommodation had once stood. Just a handful of figures were dismantling the last few tents. He climbed out and walked over to an orderly who was gathering up litter and debris strewn around.

"What's happened? Where's everyone going?" he asked.

"They've been ordered south, somewhere near Arras," replied the man.

Harry turned around and stared forlornly at the empty road behind him, the convoy out of sight. He was too late. Rose was gone.

Chapter Twenty-two

The scent of lavender drifted across the road and Harry
was instantly back in the *manoir* garden with Rose. All
the things they had said to each other that day, the
promises they'd made. Had those meant nothing to her?
Was she thinking about him now? Or was she thinking
about a different soldier? He cursed his own lack of
action and now it was too late. Their paths would
probably never cross again.

A shout jolted him from his reverie. "Harry. Are you
listening?" He looked round at Arthur who was knee-
deep in muddy water next to his ambulance which was
sitting nose-first in a large ditch running alongside the
main canal. Arthur had been returning to headquarters
when a child emerged from behind a cart and tottered into
the road. He'd had no option but to swerve and the car
had pitched into the channel, a wave of ditch water
gushing into the cab.

"Yes, course I'm listening. We need a tow rope," said
Harry.

Arthur threw his hands in the air. "I just said that."

A small crowd had formed, watching the drama unfold
and waiting to see what *les anglais* were going to do.
Harry turned to the onlookers. "Anyone have a rope?
Une corde, s'il vous plaît?"

An elderly man wearing a grubby jacket and cap
raised his hand and indicated to Harry to wait. He
disappeared into one of the nearby houses and returned
moments later carrying a length of neatly coiled rope.

"*Merci, Monsieur,*" said Harry, taking the rope. The
man smiled, revealing a mouth full of blackened teeth.
Harry manoeuvred his car, so it was back-to-back with
the stranded ambulance. Arthur attached one end of the
rope to his vehicle and tied the other to Harry's. He

stopped by the cab and delved into his breast pocket, pulling out the photograph of Flo and the children. "Hang on to this for me. Don't want it to get wet if I end up in the drink."

Harry tucked it away and waited for Arthur to wade through the water and scrabble into his cab. He slowly edged forward until the rope was taut and he felt resistance. The engine revved and the wheels started spinning. The elderly man shouted encouragement.

"*Allez, allez!*"

Harry gently pressed the accelerator. He felt the resistance again and then a hint of movement.

"*Oui, oui. C'est ça. Allez!*" The man waved his arm.

He pressed his foot down and the car advanced slightly. The engine screamed in protest, but he could feel it nudging forward. He pressed down harder, and it appeared to gather momentum. For a moment the wheels started spinning again and then suddenly it was free and the crowd was cheering. Arthur hopped down and ran his sleeve across his brow.

"I wasn't sure our plan was going to work."

Harry slapped him on the back. "Never doubted it for a moment."

***

The men arrived at headquarters to find the camp strangely deserted. Captain Bate must have been looking out for them as he was scurrying over before Harry had climbed down from his cab.

"Don't bother getting out, Private Stone," barked the captain. "Where have you been?"

"Sorry, Sir. Had to rescue Private Richards' car from a ditch."

"Is it damaged?" asked Bate.

"No, Sir."

Arthur appeared at the captain's side. "A child ran out in front of me, Sir."

"Right well, we've had orders to attend the dressing station in Strazeele. All hell has broken loose, by all accounts. Drop off at No. 15 Clearing Station in Ebblinghem. The convoy's already on its way."

"Right, Sir."

Bate turned on his heels and hurried away. Arthur looked down at his sodden breeches. "Bugger. I was hoping to dry these out."

***

Strazeele lay thirteen miles northeast. Progress was painfully slow, hampered by the endless line of refugees flooding away from the advancing Germans. Harry surveyed the dirty and bedraggled procession of mainly women and children, a few elderly men dotted amongst them. Some were pushing carts or prams loaded with their possessions. Most of the children were carrying a small case or bag. They were heading west to the coast, but Harry wondered how many of them would manage to secure passage across the Channel.

Arthur was up ahead, and Harry saw him hop out of his cab to assist a woman who had slipped over in the mud. She had two young children in tow. He helped her to her feet and retrieved her case. The woman ushered her children back into the trudging mass of weary bodies.

It was over two hours before they crawled into Strazeele. Harry had witnessed many places in ruins but nowhere had ever felt this desolate and bleak. The town had been ravaged, homes and shops reduced to mounds of bricks and shattered planks of wood. A wall remained here and there, standing defiantly amongst the devastation. He passed the remains of a windmill balanced on a pile of rubble. The sails were no more than stumps, ripped away like limbs from a body. The only sign of life was a solitary tree rising incongruously from the wasteland.

The dressing station had been established in a small field on the outskirts of the village. A convoy of horse-drawn ambulances were carrying casualties from the front line. He pulled up behind Arthur and climbed down. The ground shook as a shell exploded just a short distance away, and Harry watched the field erupt in a mass of earth and shrapnel. The horses started whinnying and a couple of them were rearing and fighting against their harnesses. He shivered, as if an icy finger had run down his back. A hand landed on his shoulder, making him start. It was Arthur.

"They're going to have to move back and relocate the dressing station. The shelling's getting too close."

Harry nodded and the two of them ducked as another blast ripped through a small wood a hundred yards to their right.

"U.B.C," said Arthur, wryly. "See you at No. 15."

Harry moved round to the rear of his vehicle where a stream of orderlies carrying stretchers had emerged. For the first time, Harry could see fear in their faces. No quips, no banter.

A succession of shells bombarded the area once again and he could hear a medical officer yelling instructions to pack up and withdraw. With his car loaded, he leapt in and nervously waited for the last casualty to be stowed in Arthur's vehicle.

The next moment a deafening roar filled his ears and everything in front of him disappeared in a thunderous boom. Debris came showering down, thudding on the roof and windscreen. He could hear shouting and screaming, and he froze in horror as he realised Arthur and his car had disappeared in a cloud of smoke and wreckage. Time slowed down and the noises became muffled as if he were underwater. His limbs felt like lead as he fell from the cab and stared at the scene before him. The smoke began to drift away. He rushed forward only to feel a hand grab his arm and pull him back.

"Get back in your car, Private!" roared a voice.

"But Sir…"

"We'll see to them. Get in your ambulance and get those casualties out of here."

Harry couldn't move, his head swimming.

"Now!" bellowed the fuming officer. The two men jumped as another shell landed nearby, spraying soil and fragments. Harry clambered into his cab and, taking one last look at the mangled wreckage, slowly pulled away. Hands shaking, he fumbled in his pocket for a cigarette, but his fingers touched something else, and he realised he still had Arthur's photograph.

Chapter Twenty-three

Saint Omer was bathed in spring warmth, sunlight bouncing off the creamy stonework and filling the streets with a dazzling brightness. After more than twelve months of living in the harsh conditions of a clearing station, Rose was pleased to be back in the familiar town. She raised her face to the sun and let her skin soak up the morning heat.

Turning to peer through the patisserie window, she could see Amy in full flow, buying what appeared to be most of the shop. Love and affection for her friend flowed through her. What would she have done without her? Amy had helped her to put that day in the woods behind her and even though an occasional nightmare woke her in the early hours, the anxiety had diminished. She had also begun to accept that the future she had envisaged with Harry was lost. She had no idea why and perhaps would never know.

A minute later Amy emerged onto the pavement with an armful of small boxes each tied with blue ribbon.

"How many have you bought? We'll never eat all those," said Rose, relieving her of three of the parcels.

"I thought I'd treat everyone and there are two giant eclairs for you and me. Let's find somewhere to sit."

It was Saturday and the town square was alive with the bustle of market day. Clucking hens were packed into wooden crates and squealing piglets scrabbled round in makeshift pens. The two women strolled through the crowds. They passed a trestle table laden with velvety rabbits stretched out in a lifeless pose, their glassy eyes staring into space. Rose jumped as a young pig shrieked in her ear. She turned to see it hanging round the shoulders of a burly local, held fast by its legs and screeching in protest. Dozens of eggs were stacked in neat rows, tiny feathers still adorning them. The animals were beginning to bake in the heat and a couple of times Rose covered her nose to stem the pungent odour.

Amy pointed at a low wall near the fountain where they could perch. As they feasted on the rich pastry, Rose studied the dark green statue of a child and a swan. It sat above a shallow pool surrounded by sandy-coloured cobblestones. She found it captivating. It seemed to encapsulate the innocence and beauty of childhood and she wondered who had designed it. Her eye was drawn to a figure in uniform waving at them and she nudged Amy.

"Look, it's your Canadian sweetheart."

Amy looked up at the soldier now making his way through the throng.

"*Ooh la la*," said Rose.

"Shh," said Amy, colour rising to her cheeks.

"*Bonjour, mademoiselles*." The soldier removed his cap and gave a little bow. His dark hair was slicked back and neatly parted. Friendly eyes and a broad smile lit up his face.

"*Bonjour*," replied Amy, quickly wiping a dob of cream from the corner of her mouth.

"*Bonjour, Monsieur*," said Rose. There was an awkward silence and Rose looked from the soldier, fiddling with his cap, to Amy, twiddling a stray lock of hair.

"Well, I better be off. I'll see you back on the ward, Amy? *Au revoir, Monsieur*." She stood and gathered up the boxes and Amy flashed her a grateful smile. As she crossed the square, she stole a backward glance and was delighted to see the soldier had taken a seat on the wall and he and Amy were deep in conversation.

***

Rose deposited the cakes in the nurses' room and hurried back to her ward. She made an excuse for Amy's tardiness, eliciting a tut from the Duty Sister, and commenced her duties, enjoying the warm greeting she received from the patients.

It was only moments later when a shout went up announcing imminent casualties and she hastened to join the party waiting by the doors to the courtyard. The first ambulance trundled through the archway and orderlies stepped forward. Rose was awaiting instructions from the medical officer when Amy appeared at her side, eyes sparkling and cheeks flushed.

"Just in time," whispered Rose. The nurses accompanied the new arrivals to the wards and swiftly set to work. She had just finished attending to her first patient when Amy beckoned her over. Standing beside a bunk containing a heavily bandaged figure, crimson stains seeping through the dressings, she said in a hushed voice, "His pulse is very weak. Will you help me change his dressings?"

"Of course," replied Rose, but as she knelt, she froze.

"What is it?" asked Amy, staring at her in alarm.

Rose could barely speak. "It's Arthur."

***

The women removed Arthur's stained tunic and breeches and gently washed him down before changing his dressings. He was semi-conscious and quiet, except for an occasional cry or groan. The medical officer arrived to administer a dose of morphine and in answer to Rose's questioning look, gave a little shake of his head. She watched Arthur drift in and out of sleep, her heart breaking for the family waiting at home. She and Amy moved on to the next patient, but every so often, Rose glanced over at him, fearful that his chest would no longer be rising and falling.

***

By early evening, every casualty had been washed and treated and those able to eat, had been given mutton stew and a mug of strong tea. The ward was tranquil with just the hushed tone of a nurse reassuring a restless patient. Rose had grabbed a snack and hastily returned to sit at Arthur's bedside. His eyes remained closed, and he was mumbling incoherently.

As twilight approached, she could see through the window a full moon rising above the rooftops, like a white balloon floating on an inky pond. She caught the sound of a clock in the distance chiming ten. A moment later a bell started ringing and someone shouted "The Taubes are coming!" Rose could hear the ominous drone of enemy aircraft. The staff leapt into action, opening windows to reduce the impact of a blast, and placing pillows where the patients could protect their faces from flying glass. The lights were extinguished, and they waited.

The engines grew louder and within minutes the first bomb landed. The ground shook and the windows rattled. Arthur's eyes opened wide in panic and Rose knelt to take his hand.

"Arthur, it's Rose." His eyes found hers and the panic was replaced with confusion. "You're in Saint Omer, in the hospital."

Another bomb dropped and a flurry of plaster wafted to the floor. She felt his grip tighten round her fingers. "Try to drink some water." She held a mug to his lips and lifted his head. As he lay back down, a weak smile crossed his face.

"Rose."

"Hello, Arthur." She returned the smile and squeezed his hand. "How are you feeling?"

"Oh, I've had worse days." His voice was low and raspy.

"Do you remember what happened?"

"Not really…is Harry alright?"

"There were a lot of casualties but no other drivers." The two of them jumped as another explosion rocked the building.

"You wouldn't have a cigarette, would you?"

"I'll get one."

She picked her way between the bunks towards the nurses' station and returned with a cigarette and a box of matches. Arthur's face was pale and drawn, beads of perspiration glistening on his brow. The skies had gone quiet but shouts from the street echoed round the ward and Rose could see the glow of a burning building illuminating the darkness outside. The next bombardment would begin soon. She held the cigarette for Arthur to draw on.

"Harry's going to need you when all this is over," he said.

Rose gave him a puzzled look. "But I haven't seen or heard from him in months."

"That's because he saw you with your other sweetheart."

"My what?"

"He saw you with a soldier. Giving you flowers."

She wracked her brain, and then with a sinking feeling, realised what Harry must have witnessed. No wonder he never came back to see her.

"He wasn't my sweetheart. Just someone saying, 'thank you'," she said quietly.

"You have to find him and tell him," Arthur said. "He

deserves to be happy, and you can help him to see that."
He held his breath and winced as a bolt of pain shot
through him.

Rose mopped the sweat trickling down his face. "I'm
going to fetch the MO," she said, kneeling up, but he
grasped her hand.

"No, stay. Stay with me, please. Will you do
something for me?"

"Of course."

"In one of my pockets, there's a silver cigarette case.
Will you give it to Harry? I want him to have it." His
breathing was shallow, and Rose brushed a tear from her
cheek.

"I'll make sure he gets it."

"Wish I could have seen the little 'uns grow up."

"You will, Arthur, you will. You'll be back in Blighty
before you know it."

He looked at her and gave a little smile. "Harry's a
good man. I know you'll have a wonderful life together."

She nodded, unable to speak, the tears flowing freely
now.

"But you can tell him, he's a bloomin' awful card
player."

She heard the rumble of planes returning and glanced
up at the window. The ground trembled as the first bomb
fell. She turned back to Arthur and knew that he had
gone. With a sob, she closed his eyelids and pulled the
sheet over his face.

Chapter Twenty-four

Harry lay on his bunk, alone in the tent. Grief was so familiar to him, like a recurring injury. It was a physical pain, visceral and penetrating. He had watched Lieutenant Kerr collect Arthur's belongings and pack them into a crate, ready to be sent home to his family. Did Florence even know yet? Was she carrying on with daily life, blissfully unaware? He couldn't bear to see Arthur's empty bunk stripped down to the flimsy mattress. Just another piece of anonymous army kit. A pack of cards had been found tucked away, which Harry had requested to keep. He stowed them with Arthur's photograph. Something tangible to hold on to. His mind was a maelstrom of thoughts. Arthur. And Rose. Was she still in Arras? Did she love someone else?

Dev appeared and perched on Harry's bed. "They're about to start," he said. He patted Harry's arm and passed him his cap. "Let's go."

***

The men of No 2 Convoy formed a sombre gathering, Captain Bate and the chaplain standing in front of them. The day was dry and bright with a light breeze. Harry and Dev joined the assembly and Bate stepped forward.

"We stand here today to commemorate and give thanks for the life of Private Arthur Richards." The captain cleared his throat and took a moment to compose himself.

"Private Richards was a dedicated and hard-working soldier who carried out his duties with diligence and fortitude. He was a man of compassion and gallantry with sound judgement and a common-sense approach to army life. His cheery disposition and sense of humour made for good company and his talents as a card player were legendary. I believe there are very few of you who haven't been relieved of a cigarette or two by Private Richards' card skills."

A soft laugh rippled through the group.

"Private Richards was a soldier and a gentleman, and I can say with confidence he will be greatly missed by one and all." The captain paused. "We will be toasting Private Richards this evening and to that end, I have procured additional rations of rum. I will now hand over to the Padre who will lead the prayers."

As the chaplain began the reading, Harry's mind wandered. Everything the Captain had said was true. But to Harry, Arthur had been so much more. For three years, from their very early days at training camp together, Arthur had been the voice of reason. A guiding light. It dawned on Harry that Arthur had in fact been his saviour.

The service ended with the Lord's Prayer and a minute's silence, broken only by the distant thud of shells and artillery. As the rest of the men dispersed, Frank, Dev and Billy gathered round Harry and reached for their cigarettes. Harry caught Frank studying him.

"I'm alright, Frank. Really," he said.

"This bloody war," said the big man.

"Our lads are up against it, now the Boche have reinforcements from the East," said Dev.

"We *are* going to win though, aren't we?" asked Billy.

"Course we are," said Frank. "Don't you ever doubt it."

"At least the Yanks have turned up now," said Dev.

"Better late than never," muttered Harry.

"Yes, we can all sleep safe in our beds now the Doughboys are here," said Frank.

The sound of engines starting up drew their attention.

"Time to go, lads," said Frank, flicking his cigarette to

the ground. "Let's make a good job, eh? For Arthur."

The other three nodded. "For Arthur."

"For Arthur," said Billy.

Chapter Twenty-five

It was the beginning of June, and the men were awaiting the day's orders. Captain Bate emerged from his tent and walked over.

"We're collecting patients from No. 8 Clearing Station in Wavrans and delivering to No. 4 Stationary Hospital in Arques."

Harry's heart took a leap. No 8? He glanced at Dev who returned his look with raised eyebrows.

"Wavrans is twenty miles south-west of here. Study the map. Carry on."

Harry grabbed Dev's arm. "No 8. Do you think Rose is still with No 8?"

"There's only one way to find out," replied Dev, grinning.

***

The clearing station was situated in a pasture on the outskirts of Wavrans, a pretty village nestling in undulating countryside and bordered by a picturesque river that meandered north to the sea.

Harry pulled into the station with a mixture of nerves and excitement. He knew he wouldn't have the opportunity to go in search of Rose but who knows, she could just be passing by as they were loading up. After scanning the face of every nurse nearby as the stretchers were stowed, he hurriedly questioned one and received the answer he'd hoped for. Rose was there. His heart soared.

"Would you like me to pass on a message to her?" asked the nurse.

"Yes. Yes, please. Tell her Harry is looking for her and …" Harry thought for a moment. "I'll come back when I've dropped off these patients and I'll wait here for her, say, in three hours."

"I'll tell her."

"Thank you. Thank you so much." He leant forward and gave the nurse a peck on the cheek causing her to blush and as she hastened away, he threw his cap in the air and let out a whoop.

***

The journey to Arques seemed to take an eternity, the roads as congested as ever. At least the dry weather had improved driving conditions. The scene outside the hospital was busy but well-organised. It was a long wait, so Harry stood at the rear of his car, chatting to the patients, all the while his stomach churning with anticipation. He handed out cigarettes to the appreciative men and told some jokes he'd heard the day before.

Eventually they moved up the line. Harry wished the men luck and climbed in the cab. He took the road back to Wavrans, his nerves building with every mile. Would she be there? Did she still love him? Or had she given her heart to someone else?

***

He saw her waiting for him, standing in the sunshine. With shaking hands, he parked the car and climbed out. She saw him and watched as he walked towards her. Wrapping her in his arms, he held her as if he was never going to let her go. He could feel her clinging to him and when they eventually parted her eyes were wet with tears. He took her face in his hands and kissed her tenderly on the lips. A couple of passing soldiers whistled and cheered. Wiping the tears from her face, he kissed her again.

"I can't believe you're here," she said. "I thought I'd never see you again."

"I only found out this morning that No 8 was back in the area." He took her hand. "Shall we find somewhere quiet?"

"Let's go to the river."

They made their way down the hill away from the camp, scrambling over a fence and weaving through a copse of trees, eventually emerging on the banks of the river. The water was flowing briskly, sparkling flecks of sunlight dancing on its surface. The trees and bushes were the vivid green of early summer and alive with birdsong. A majestic lime tree stood nearby, the intoxicating scent of its white blossom filling the air.

The two of them sunk down into the long grass and lay in each other's arms, luxuriating in each other's company. After a few minutes, Harry leant up on his elbow, his face serious. "I have to know…do you love him?"

Rose couldn't help but smile. "The soldier with the flowers, you mean? No, I don't love him."

Relief coursed through him, and he dropped back down into the grass, grinning.

"He was just saying thank you for looking after his brother. He had been at death's door, but the doctors managed to save him, and I helped to nurse him." It was Rose's turn to look serious. "I really wish you'd talked to me instead of leaving. When I didn't hear from you or see you, I thought you'd changed your mind."

"Never," said Harry, grabbing her hand.

"I only found out why you hadn't been to see me because of Arthur…"

Harry jerked up. "You saw Arthur?"

Rose met his gaze. "I was with him when he died."

"What? I thought you were in Arras?"

"I was sent back to Saint Omer for a while, before it was evacuated."

Harry lay back down. "Did you speak to him?"

"Yes." She delved into her pocket and retrieved the silver cigarette case. "He wanted you to have this."

Harry sat up and took the case. Slowly turning it over in his hands, the tears began to flow. Rose pulled him towards her and held him while he wept for his friend.

"I miss him like hell," he said eventually, wiping his eyes. "I'm glad you were with him. That he wasn't alone."

The two of them sat side by side in the sunshine, listening to the birds and thinking about Arthur, while the river flowed past on its way to the sea.

***

As the sun moved round, the branches of the lime tree threw them into shadow. Harry stood up and walked over to the trunk, rifling in his pocket.

"What are you doing?" asked Rose.

"You'll see." He dug out his penknife and began to carve.

Ten minutes later he called her over. She studied the words, tears pricking her eyes. 'Harry loves Rose' was now etched in the bark. She pointed to the trunk and said, "Perhaps you could carve 'Rose loves Harry' underneath."

***

The men were eating when Harry returned to camp. He crept in and plonked down next to Dev, receiving a questioning stare from the Lieutenant. Dev pushed a plate of potato pie towards him.

"Saved this for you."

"Excellent. Thanks." Harry tucked in.

"Well?"

"It's not bad."

"Not the pie."

Harry grinned. "She was there. We went down to the river, just beyond the camp."

Dev gave him a friendly punch on the arm.

"It's the perfect place to meet. No one around."

The men continued eating, oblivious to Carter sitting behind them.

Chapter Twenty-six

Rose awoke the following morning still glowing from the events of the previous day. Knowing that Harry loved her brought deep happiness. She pictured a future for the two of them. A wedding, a home, a family. She thought about Arthur and her heart broke for his wife and young children. Harry would be mourning his friend for a long time. She glanced over at Amy who was still sleeping, her wild hair strewn across the pillow like the tresses of a fairy tale princess.

"Amy, time to get up."

Amy pulled the covers over her head and mumbled something unintelligible. Rose felt under her bunk for one of her boots and lobbed it in her direction.

"Ow."

"Wake up, sleeping beauty."

Amy groaned and emerged from under the sheets, rubbing her face. "It can't be time to get up."

"'Fraid so. But the birds are singing and it's a sunny day."

"Oh no. You're going to be all cheerful and in love, aren't you?"

Rose climbed out of bed and picked up her washbag. "I'm sure I don't know what you mean."

Washed and dressed, she made her way to breakfast, leaving Amy to do her usual last-minute rush. Rose had long-ago abandoned the nervous wait for her. She preferred to savour her food, albeit just tea and toast. It was indeed a beautiful day, and she could feel real warmth in the air even at this early hour. She queued for her meal and, spotting the chaplain, walked over to join him.

"Good morning, Padre."

"Morning, Sister."

"Lovely day."

The chaplain studied her for a moment, picking up something in her manner. "You seem particularly bright and breezy this morning, if I may say so."

Rose smiled and sipped her tea. "Do I?"

He raised his eyebrows. "It wouldn't have anything to do with a certain ambulance driver, would it?"

Since working closely together in the Moribund tent, Rose and the chaplain had formed an unlikely bond and over the past months had become close friends. They had spent long hours discussing a myriad of topics, including faith, war, and love. Late one evening, she had even plucked up the courage to confide in him about Carter's assault.

Rose put her mug down and grabbed his hand excitedly. "Yes. I saw him yesterday."

"And?"

She took a bite of her toast and leant back, beaming. The chaplain smiled. "Ah, I see. It's love then?"

She nodded, her eyes twinkling. He patted her arm affectionately. "Well, let's hope this wretched war is over soon and the two of you can begin your lives together."

At that moment Amy arrived, out of breath and clutching her cape and cap. Rose cast a look around. "Amy, your cap. If Matron sees you…"

"I know, I know. I'll just get some tea and then I'll fix it." She threw her things on the table and rushed off. Rose shook her head. "Always a whirlwind."

"She's a free spirit who wants to help people. We could do with more people like that in the world."

Rose watched Amy trying to pin her hair with one hand, a mug of tea in the other and thought the chaplain was probably right.

***

She arrived on duty and, following a brief handover from the night staff, began her work. It was a busy shift with the ward at capacity.

Towards the end of the day, a nurse ducked into the tent and gave a wave to Rose, a piece of paper in her hand.

"I've a message for you," she said, holding out the paper for Rose to take.

"Who's it from?"

"One of the ambulance drivers. A rather attractive one." The nurse smiled and headed out. Rose noticed the Senior Sister eyeing her so slipped the note into her pocket for later, a flutter of excitement rippling through her stomach.

***

Duties completed for the day, she found a quiet space to read the message.

Managed to get a few hours leave. Meet me tomorrow at 5 o'clock at our place by the river. Harry.

Tomorrow? She'd been sure it would be days, if not weeks before they would see each other again. She pocketed the note and hurried off to tell Amy.

***

Rose clock watched the whole of the following day. Despite the heavy workload, the shift seemed to drag and five o'clock couldn't come quickly enough. It was nearer half-past five before she had permission to leave. She couldn't risk taking the time to wash her hands and face or tidy her hair. What if Harry left, thinking she couldn't make it?

She trotted across the field and over the fence. By the

time she reached the copse, she was almost running, excitement taking hold of her. She emerged from the trees and slowed to a walk. She couldn't see Harry, but his cap was lying on the ground beneath the lime tree, and she rushed forward, calling his name. She saw a flash of khaki and a figure appeared from behind the tree. But it wasn't Harry. It was Carter.

Chapter Twenty-seven

The convoy continued to transport patients to Arques, this time from No 15 Clearing Station in Ebblingham. The Allies were still suffering heavy casualties as the Germans launched their attacks, bolstered by troops arriving from the Eastern Front. Rose filled Harry's thoughts. The happiness that coursed through him helped to fill the chasm left by Arthur. His hours behind the wheel were spent planning a new life. Could it be possible there was a future for him? Did he dare believe it?

The men had endured an exhausting forty-eight hours and welcomed the chance to have a smoke in the sunshine before supper. Harry was lounging by some crates with Luc at his side. He watched a group playing cards and pictured Arthur sitting amongst them, a cigarette dangling from his lips. He closed his eyes and turned his face towards the late afternoon sun, his mind wandering.

A minute later, he heard a shout announcing the arrival of the post. The Lieutenant appeared with an armful of letters and parcels. Harry continued his reverie, knowing there wouldn't be anything for him. He was vaguely aware of names being called, one after another.

"Carter." There was no response. The officer looked around. "Where's Private Carter? Does anyone know?"

A voice spoke up. "Gone to No 8 Clearing Station, Sir."

Harry sat up.

"Said he had some business to attend to, Sir."

Dev flashed a look at him. Harry leapt up and darted over. "He's gone to find Rose, hasn't he?" he said.

"I've a horrible feeling you're right," said Dev.

"I have to go. Can you cover for me?"

"Course, mate. Go."

***

Rose stopped dead in her tracks. She couldn't make sense of what she was seeing. How could Carter be here? Then a primal fear engulfed her. She could feel her heart pounding in her chest. Carter blew out a stream of smoke and flicked the stub away.

"Hello, Rose. I believe we have some unfinished business, you and I."

She started to back away. Her brain was whirring as she tried to control the panic rising in her. She knew she couldn't outrun him and as she reached up to her bare head, she realised with horror, this time she didn't have a weapon. Carter saw the movement and gave a scornful laugh. "Oh dear, nothing to defend yourself with?"

Rose said nothing. She was breathing hard and quickly rubbed at the tears trickling down her cheeks. Carter took another step forward, a lewd smirk crossing his face. He made a lunge towards her, trying to grab her arm. Rose lashed out with as much force as she could, catching him square in the eye. He drew back his hand and struck her hard in the face. She gasped with pain and shock. She felt a shove and stumbled sideways, but when she looked round, someone else was there. Another figure in khaki. It was Harry.

She scrambled out of the way as the two men tumbled to the ground, grappling with each other in a snarl of jabs and punches, like crazed animals in a primeval battle. The men landed blow after blow on each other. Harry had never felt such fury. He tasted blood as his lip split open and he retaliated with a swipe at Carter's jaw. Carter managed to wrestle out of his grip and, scrabbling to his feet, he turned to face him, blood oozing from his nose.

"Well, well, well. The hero has come to rescue his damsel." He wiped a sleeve across his face, creating a crimson smear down his cheek.

"I told you to stay away from her," growled Harry.

"You think you've come to save her virtue, do you? Too late for that, my friend."

Harry charged towards him, eyes blazing. He launched himself and his shoulder slammed into Carter's stomach. Rose cried out as she watched the two of them stagger together as if in some ritualistic dance, then topple off the bank and into the river.

Harry surfaced, coughing and spluttering. The water was icy and moving fast, dragging him away. He hastily scanned round and spotted Carter twelve yards away clinging to a branch jutting from the riverbank. Behind the blood and dirt, a look of utter terror filled his face.

"Help me," screamed Carter, "I can't swim, I can't swim." He was clawing at the branch in a frantic attempt to get a better grip. Harry began to swim towards him, using all his strength to fight the fierce current. He was a few feet away when Carter stretched out to him, "Grab me. Grab me."

Harry reached out and was inches away, but then Carter lost his grasp. His face contorted with panic as the water swept him away and Harry watched him pirouetting in the swirling flow. Carter disappeared under the surface then reappeared briefly, one arm outstretched in a macabre wave, before disappearing for the last time.

***

The two of them were in a state of shock and disbelief. They stumbled back to the clearing station where Harry installed Rose in a corner of the mess tent nursing a mug of tea while he went in search of an officer. They were now sitting together, holding hands, and waiting. Rose was trembling and her eyes brimmed with tears.

"Do you think he drowned? He must have drowned. You said he couldn't swim. Perhaps he grabbed on to something? We should have searched."

Harry wrapped his arm around her shoulders. "It's going to be alright."

She shrugged him off and stood up, pacing back and forth, and wringing her hands. "There's something I haven't told you." Tears were rolling down her cheeks and Harry's stomach clenched into a knot as he held his breath.

"Carter attacked me."

He leapt to his feet. "What? When?"

"Last year. I had leave and I went for a walk in the woods. I don't even know how he came to be there, but he drove by while I was waiting for my lift."

Bracing himself, he asked, "Did he hurt you?"

"He was on top of me. He tried to… I couldn't get him off." Her voice trailed off and large sobs racked through her. Harry took her in his arms and waited.

"I was so scared. I didn't know what to do. Then I stabbed him with my hat pin." Rose began to ramble. "They're going to think we killed him. They'll say we took revenge. We'll be charged with murder."

Harry guided her chin so he could look directly in her eyes. "Listen to me. We're going to tell the truth and they're going to believe us." He held her close again. A movement caught his eye and he turned to see a grim-faced major and two members of the military police approaching. A minute later, he and Rose were being led through the camp, questioning stares following them all the way.

***

The following hours were a blur of unfamiliar faces repeating the same questions, sometimes the voice softly spoken and empathetic, other times aggressive. He and Rose had been separated and as Harry waited in the empty room, he pictured her alone and scared.

It was late into the night when a face he recognised finally appeared. He stood and saluted as Captain Bate entered and placed a mug of tea on the table in front of him.

"Sit down, Private."

"How's Sister Davidson, Sir?"

"She's being looked after." The captain shifted in his seat. "Private Carter's body has been found."

Harry slumped back in his seat whilst Bate continued, "Three miles downstream. Listen, Stone, the MPs have given me your version of events, but we all know there was no love lost between Private Carter and yourself. You're looking at a court martial here."

Harry felt a wave of foreboding wash over him. "It was an accident, Sir. He was attacking Rose... Sister Davidson... we fought, and we ended up in the river. I had no idea he couldn't swim."

Bate studied him for a moment then leant forward. "I believe you, Harry and naturally, I will speak on your behalf, but the MPs need to be convinced."

Harry bowed his head and tried to ignore the nausea rising from his stomach. As Bate rose from his chair, he said, "I'll go and see if I can get you released into my charge." He pointed at the mug. "Drink your tea."

Harry stood to attention. "Sir." The door closed and he dropped back down, the tea untouched.

***

He was released in the early hours of the morning and driven back to camp. Confined to quarters, he spent a torturous twenty-four hours waiting for news. His mind was in a perpetual cycle of fear for himself and fear for Rose. What if they weren't believed? Could it be possible they would face a firing squad? His overwhelming tiredness only served to exacerbate the horror of the situation. Eventually he was summoned to the captain's tent.

Bate was sitting behind his desk with the lieutenant standing nearby. Both men appeared solemn, and Kerr was visibly upset. The captain wasted no time. "It's not good news. You're going to be court martialled."

Harry's legs buckled and he grabbed the desk to steady himself.

Bate continued. "It's a charge of murder and a date has been set for two days hence."

Harry summoned all his strength to stand straight and control his breathing. "And Rose?"

"Sister Davidson been released without charge."

Harry closed his eyes as relief flooded through him. At least Rose was safe. "May I see her, Sir?"

"I'm afraid that won't be possible. You're to be transferred to Rouen immediately."

Harry's heart sank. The chances of Rose managing to reach Rouen were nigh on impossible.

The captain's tone softened. "Lieutenant Kerr and I will speak in your defence, but I must warn you, it's a Field General Court Martial, so whilst the verdict is not a certainty, Carter had friends in high places, and they are pushing for the death penalty. You must prepare yourself."

***

186

As Harry awaited trial, he paced the locked room hour after hour, his head a tangle of thoughts and emotions. He had barely eaten, and despite his exhaustion, sleep eluded him. How did it ever come to this? The idea of never seeing Rose again haunted him day and night.

That evening, Captain Bate appeared.

"How're you holding up, Private?" he asked.

"Fine, thank you, Sir."

"Right, well, the court martial is at ten hundred hours tomorrow and ..." Bate broke off as the door opened and an officer entered carrying a sheaf of papers and a chair.

"Ah, Captain," said Bate, then turned to Harry. "Captain Livingstone has been appointed as your Defending Officer."

Harry saluted as the man placed the chair down and dropped the papers on to the desk.

"Sorry we're not meeting under better circumstances, Private. Now, take a seat, we've a lot to get through. The first thing I must tell you is the court has refused permission to call Sister Davidson as a witness. It would appear the victim's family has a powerful sphere of influence."

The three men huddled around the tiny desk and began the slow process of preparing for trial. It was after two in the morning before the officers departed and Harry was left alone, staring at the wall, terror clutching at him. He thought of Rose. Ten minutes later, he requested a pen and paper.

***

Rose had returned to camp filled with an excruciating mix of relief for her release and horror at what was facing Harry. What if they found him guilty? Her mind raced with images of him in front of a firing squad. It was too much to bear. She had to do something. There had to be someone who could help. And then it came to her.

**

Shortly before ten the following morning, Harry was escorted to a wooden building on the far side of the base. He stepped inside and immediately spotted Kerr and Bate, who gave him an encouraging nod. Livingstone was standing to the right and three officers were seated behind a long desk. Harry stood to attention and saluted. The officer sitting in the middle cleared his throat and commenced the proceedings.

"Private Harold Stone MT145678 Mechanical Transport, Army Service Corps, attached to 2nd Motor Ambulance Convoy, Royal Army Medical Corps, you are charged with wilfully and purposely causing the death by drowning of Private Edward Carter MT257839 on the 29th of June 1918. How do you plead?"

"Not guilty, Sir."

"Major Peters, Officer for the Prosecution, you may proceed."

Peters was a stick-thin man in his early fifties with a thick moustache and receding hair. He eyed Harry with pure contempt as the cross-examination began.

"Private Stone, do you admit that your relationship with Private Carter was one of antagonism from the start?"

"I objected to his treatment of one of our mechanics, Sir."

"Just answer the question, Private."

"Yes, Sir."

"Do you admit, Private Stone, that on the 17th of June 1916, you were absent without leave for ten hours?"

"Yes, Sir."

"And would you like to explain to the court the reason for this."

"My dog had been run over and needed urgent medical treatment."

"Run over, you say? By what?"

"One of the ambulance cars."

"And who was driving this ambulance car?"

Harry glanced at Bate, "Private Carter."

Peters cast a look at the three officers behind the desk, then continued, "And do you also admit that on the 24th of November 1916 you carried out an unprovoked attack on Private Carter, resulting in him sustaining a broken nose?"

"Carter was making inappropriate comments about one of the nurses, Sir."

"Ah, yes. Sister Davidson. Your partner in crime."

Harry bristled and Bate shot him a warning glance.

"I put it to the court that on the date in question you went in search of Private Carter with the sole aim of seeking revenge by ending his life."

"No…I was protecting Rose…Sister Davidson…"

"Don't interrupt, Private," barked one of the officers. A sarcastic smile crossed Peters lips.

"You were intent on causing Private Carter harm and when you pushed him into the river and realised, he was unable to swim, the deed was done."

"That's not what happened…I tried to save him."

"You will be in contempt if you interrupt again, Private."

As the realisation hit, an intense fear twisted Harry's guts. The verdict was a foregone conclusion. Carter's uncle had wielded his power and the true details of what had happened were now irrelevant. By the time Captain Livingstone was asked to call his witnesses, Harry knew his fate was sealed. Bate and Kerr delivered their statements, while the men who held his life in their hands, shuffled papers and paid scant attention.

How he managed to deliver his own testimony and answer Livingstone's questions, Harry had no idea. He was in a living nightmare. He listened to the closing arguments and braced himself for the verdict. Suddenly the hush of the courtroom was broken by the sound of raised voices outside. Someone was demanding to enter. There was a scuffle and a shout. A moment later, the door swung open and a tall figure wearing the collar of an army chaplain strode in.

Chapter Twenty-eight

Rouen
June 1918

My dearest Rose,
I have been assured this letter will reach you, but how quickly I do not know. I am to face a court martial this very morning, which, by all accounts, is leaning heavily towards a guilty verdict. And we both know what that means.

There was a time when I would have welcomed death, but fate brought you to me and the minute I looked into your beautiful eyes, I was captivated. You helped to mend my broken heart and show me the possibility of a new life, a second chance.

But forces have conspired against us, sweet Rose, and I fear the future we planned is not to be. Be strong, my love, and be certain that, should the worst happen, you will be my final thought in this world.
Forever yours,
Harry

Rose let out a wail and crumpled to the ground. She covered her face with her hands and sobbed until there were no tears left.

***

In the camp, Frank, Billy, and Dev were gathered in silence, still trying to absorb the terrible news. Luc was lying at Dev's feet but every few minutes he would sit up and look around.

"It's alright, boy," said Dev, giving him a stroke.

"I don't understand. How could this have happened?"

said Frank. "Everyone knew Carter was a bastard."

"Yes, but with a powerful uncle," said Dev.

Billy wiped his eyes. "First Arthur, now Harry."

Frank patted his shoulder. A voice rang out. "Time to go, lads." The three men rose to their feet and donned their caps. Dev looked at Luc. "Come on, boy. You're with me now."

***

Two days later, Dev was returning to camp with Luc sitting beside him. Whilst the dog was a constant reminder of Harry's absence, Dev was grateful for his company and felt an increasing attachment and fondness towards him. He parked up alongside the other ambulances, tired and hungry as usual.

As he stepped down, a breathless Billy came rushing towards him.

"Harry's been freed. Harry's been freed," he shouted. He reached Dev and shook him by the shoulders, his face alight and eyes gleaming. "Did you hear me? Harry's alive."

Dev stared at him, hearing the words but unable to take them in.

"Isn't it the best news?" Billy was dancing with excitement. As the realisation hit, Dev's mouth widened into a broad grin.

"What happened?"

"The chaplain from Rose's clearing station intervened at the trial." Billy was hopping from foot to foot. "He confirmed Harry's version of events. Apparently, Carter had already attacked Rose once, but she managed to escape…remember that wound he had on his face last year?"

"That was Rose?" said Dev.

192

"Yep. Anyway, he tried again and that's when he and Harry got into a fight."

Dev spotted Frank running over, calling to them. "Is it true?"

"It's true. It's true," said Billy.

Luc had picked up on the excitement and was jumping between their legs, his tail whipping the air. Dev bent down. "He's coming back, boy. Harry's coming home."

***

For three days, Rose had been going about her duties whilst trying to hide the flood of grief engulfing her. She continued to work long after her shift was over and came on duty earlier than necessary. Anything to occupy her time and avoid the pain that consumed her when she was alone. Her eyes were red raw from crying and her face pale and drawn. She was grateful the patients didn't ask any questions.

Having been ordered to take a break, she emerged from the ward tent into bright sunshine. She rested her sore eyes and paused a moment to take in a breath of the warm air. Feeling tears welling, she fought them back and opened her eyes. As she turned, she stopped in her tracks. Walking towards her was someone the image of Harry. Her stomach lurched and she thought how cruel grief could be, playing tricks on her tortured mind. She watched as the figure came nearer and the face that looked like Harry's broke into a smile. Her hands came up to her mouth and she cried out in disbelief. A moment later, Harry's arms wrapped around her, and lifted her off her feet. Now it was tears of pure joy pouring down her cheeks.

"Is it you? How is this possible? Your letter…"

Harry placed his finger on her lips. "I'll explain

everything, but first…" He leant down and kissed her. A kiss filled with the love of a man who thought his life was over but had been given a second chance.

***

The following weeks saw the course of the war turn and victory for the Allies was in sight. On a freezing night in November, Harry, Dev, Frank, and Billy were crouching beside a blazing bonfire, their faces glowing in the amber light, contemplating another harsh winter ahead of them. Suddenly, they heard a commotion and the sound of cheering. They looked at each other as someone shouted, "The war's over." Another voice was calling, "The Jerries have surrendered."

The men leapt up and Harry almost toppled backwards as Frank grabbed him and hugged him until he couldn't breathe. He could hear laughing and whooping echoing through the camp. Frank released him and moved onto Billy, who was standing grinning, tears running down his face. More men joined them and there was handshaking and backslapping. A bottle of rum appeared from nowhere and was passed from man to man. Soon there was a crowd, singing and dancing around the fire.

As the news sunk in, Harry flopped down and lit a cigarette. He wished Arthur was there with them. Someone nudged his arm. It was Dev.

"What are you going to do when you get home? Apart from marry Rose of course."

"Look for work, hopefully as a driver. You?"

"Going back to the estate. The family said my job would be waiting for me."

"That's good."

Frank and Billy sank down next to them, their cheeks flushed with the alcohol.

"How about you, Frank? What are you going to do back in Blighty?" asked Dev.

Frank said loudly, "I'm going to take my savings and open an ironmongery on Dudley High Street." Swaying slightly, he put his arm around Billy's shoulders. "And Billy Billy here is going to come and work for me, aren't you mate?"

Billy just beamed and nodded. Frank drew an imaginary line in the air. "Wilson's — Dudley's Finest Ironmongers'."

Harry and Dev exchanged a smile. "That sounds great, Frank. And for you too, Billy."

"Can't wait. Can't wait."

The four friends huddled round the fire, listening to the sounds of celebration around them and wondering if they'd be home for Christmas.

***

It was mid-December when Harry found himself leaning on the ship's railings, Luc sitting at his feet. He watched Boulogne fade into the distance and pictured the thousands of soldiers who would never come home, resting for ever in foreign soil.

Retrieving Arthur's silver case from his pocket, he turned it over in his hands before opening it and picking out a cigarette. He had made the decision to return the case to Flo, along with the family photograph. It was where they belonged. He was briefly aware of a presence at his shoulder and for a moment he thought he heard Arthur's voice asking if he fancied a game of cards.

Epilogue

Reading
June 1920

It was another blisteringly hot day. Harry could feel the sun scorching the back of his head and he pulled a handkerchief from his pocket to wipe the perspiration from his neck and brow. He gazed up at the dazzling sky, not a single cloud interrupting the cornflower blue. With the final delivery completed, he slammed the van doors shut, allowing the distinctive livery to display its message once more. He hopped into the cab and eased into the crocodile of vehicles and carts. After a week of high temperatures, the road was dry and dusty and he could smell the horses, hauling their heavy loads in the summer heat.

Ten minutes later he found himself trailing a van identical to his own, the bold lettering on the rear doors enticing the discerning shopper to visit Heelas. He would be forever grateful for their offer of work, and he was acutely aware he was one of the lucky ones, at a time when thousands of demobilized men were competing for just a handful of jobs.

The leading van pulled into the goods yard with Harry close behind. They joined a neat row of delivery lorries parked parallel to each other. An image of muddy ambulance cars flashed before him and for a moment, he was back in Merville with the sound of the wounded crying and his uniform smeared with blood. It almost felt like a dream now, like it never really happened. The suffering, the death, the loss.

He spotted Sutherland, the squat foreman, noting their return on his clipboard. Harry knew he had served in Mesopotamia and seen action at Gallipoli, but like most returning soldiers, shied away from any conversation on such topics. He ran a tight ship but was well-liked and respected amongst his staff.

Harry dropped down and crossed the yard, the late afternoon sun transforming the cobbles into a mosaic of reds and browns. He placed the keys in Sutherland's waiting hand.

"Everything go smoothly today, Harry?"

"Yes, Mr Sutherland."

"Right, get yourself off. See you in the morning, bright and early."

"Yes, Sir. Cheerio."

He made his way out into the city streets, eager to be home. The shops had finished trading for the day and the pavements were clear except for a few stragglers soaking up the sunshine. Harry snaked in between them until he was free to quicken his pace.

Half an hour later, he was slotting his key into the front door. He heard a bark and before the door was half open, a furry muzzle appeared.

"Hello, boy." He knelt down while Luc fussed around him. "We'll go throw a ball in the park, shall we, eh?"

Straightening himself up, he removed his cap, tossing it expertly onto the hat stand. He paused for a moment to study the wedding photograph mounted on the wall, Mary smiling back at him. The sadness still ached inside him, but time had healed the raw grief. He brushed his fingers across the image. Sweet dreams.

Peering through to the kitchen, he watched Rose lazily stirring a spoon round a large pan on the range. Her face was flushed from the heat of the stove, the normally faint scar on her cheek a little more conspicuous. Cradled in her left arm was a sleeping baby, a bundle of creamy skin and pink cheeks. Harry stepped forward and Rose looked up, a tired smile lighting up her face.

"You're home."

"How is he?" He kissed Rose on the cheek.

"He's doing fine. Catching up on the sleep he missed out on last night."

"Here, I'll take him."

Rose transferred the infant into his arms, and she reached up to give Harry a peck.

"We've had a letter from Amy. She says Quebec is a wonderful city and apparently her in-laws adore her."

"That doesn't surprise me one bit. Have I time to go to the park before supper? Thought I'd walk with the pram and take Luc. You could put your feet up?"

"That sounds nice." She stroked the baby's cheek. "He's not long been fed so he should sleep."

"Perfect."

He stepped out of the back door and gently laid his son in the waiting pram. Luc was bouncing around the yard with excitement. Unlatching the gate, Harry negotiated the narrow passageway between the houses and a minute later the three of them were making their way up the street in the evening sun. Harry, Luc, and Arthur.

Acknowledgements

Since my teenage years I have dreamed of writing a novel, but it is only now I have finally put pen to paper. Though a solitary occupation, the result has only been possible because of the boundless support and encouragement I have received from family and friends. Below are the people who helped to make my dream come true.

My thanks go to Gill Mitchinson and Sarah Everard for their feedback on the first draft. Thank you to David Wiggins at The Museum of Military Medicine for helping me in the early stages of research. Thanks also to Janine Jackson and John Whiting for taking the time to read and comment on the second draft. Thank you to Claire Voet and the team at Blossom Spring Publishing for giving me the opportunity to see my words in print. A huge thank you to Issy Singleton whose full and detailed notes allowed me to finish my story.

Last, but by no means least, my love and heartfelt gratitude go to my family, whose unwavering enthusiasm for this venture has kept me on track: to my son, Isaac, for setting me on the right path, to my daughter, Georgia, who insisted the dog didn't die, and to my husband, Mark, who never stopped believing in me.

About the Author

Karen has spent much of her life in North Yorkshire and the city of York has been home for many years. After graduating with a degree in Modern Languages, she spent several years abroad working in Paris and Spain, before returning to the UK where she married and raised a family. In 2014 she established a coffee shop in her home village and since then has built it into a thriving business at the heart of the community.

Karen had a long-held dream to write a novel, but it was only when lockdown afforded her the time that she finally put pen to paper. With a keen interest in family history, she was eager to tell the story of her Great Grandfather, who served as an ambulance driver in France and Flanders during the First World War. The result was her debut novel 'Soldier without a Gun'.

Karen is planning a sequel and a children's book.

www.blossomspringpublishing.com